Stray
Shot

Also by Gerald Hammond:

STRAY SHOT

Gerald Hammond

St. Martin's Press
New York

Library of Congress Cataloging-in-Publication Data

Hammond, Gerald.
    Stray shot / Gerald Hammond.
        p.   cm.
    ISBN 0-312-03435-0
    I. Title.
    PR6058.A55456S7   1989
    823'.914—dc20   89-34941
                                                                  CIP

First published in Great Britain by Macmillan London Limited.

First U.S. Edition

10 9 8 7 6 5 4 3 2 1

I am deeply grateful to my friend and shooting companion, Earl H. Bell, who showed me Texas, gave inestimable help with the dialogue and then was pleased to be used as one of the characters in this book.

All other characters are as fictitious as I could make them.

G.H.

ONE

Hunger, added to a stiffness about the neck and shoulders, brought me back into the here and now. My watch said 2.35. It was daylight, so it must be early afternoon and I had missed lunch again. Absently, I transferred the contents of the word processor to disc, started the printer and wandered through into the kitchen.

Alice was there, looking, as always, fresh and feminine and irresistible. Sometimes I wondered how it was that the cottage was not eternally besieged by the entire male population of the world, all baying like hounds and trying to fight their way inside. She was doing something with food.

'I heard the printer start up,' she said.

'Yes.' I focussed on her. 'Did I hear the doorbell? Or was it part of what I was writing?'

'Keith was here.'

'Who?'

'Keith Calder,' Alice said patiently. She was used by now to my disorientation after an intense bout of writing. 'Your friend. The man you've probably been writing about all morning.'

I nodded. I knew who Keith was now. 'What did he want?'

'He said he'll come back. I said that I expected you to surface before much longer. Four hours is usually your limit. He took Boss for a walk.'

'Not before you made him spill the beans,' I said. 'I know you. Tell me all.'

Alice is too well balanced to be upset by allusions to her feminine curiosity. She put a snack on the table and almost pushed me into a chair. She had bought a small freezer and a microwave with her own money so that she could pander to my irregular eating habits. 'He wants you to go and help him on Friday. That's the day after tomorrow,' she added helpfully.

'Can I spare the time?'

'Only you know whether you're at a point where you can break off. But you've earned a holiday. I don't know much about writers, but Sir Peter says you've become amazingly prolific.'

That was probably true. Since moving in with me, Alice had relieved me of the need for almost any thought outside of my writing. Whole days which, back in London, would have been eaten up by the niggling trivia of living could now be given over to the enchanting, demanding, brain-wrenching compulsion to play with words.

'I could have the first draft finished in another day,' I said. I pushed my plate away and took an apple from the bowl. 'A break might do me good. I'll go and meet Keith.' It only dawned on me later that she had avoided telling me what help Keith was asking.

The printer had stopped. I checked that the disc contained a faithful reproduction of my morning's work and switched everything off before heading for the back door. Alice popped out of the kitchen to make sure that I had remembered to put on a jacket, but my wits were returning and I was wearing a coat and cap. She nodded approvingly. Very occasionally her guise as a self-appointed nanny irritates me, but in the main I accept, even welcome it. Usually, I need nannying.

The day was cold and shadowed. Beyond the back garden lay a wood where Sir Peter's pheasants scattered at my approach. I had come to terms with the knowledge that they were destined for the pot, but any which cared to take refuge in my garden when the sound of the beaters approached could count on a safe haven, even if they were sometimes hard on the vegetables. A sharp wind was taking the last few golden leaves off the trees and whisking them aimlessly around.

When I had first transplanted myself from London, it had been strange and humbling to have a dog at my side, attentive to my orders and wholly dependent on my whims for its food and even life. Now, so soon after, with Boss only a minute away, I felt a pang of solitude and hurried my pace. The ground rose beyond the wood. Soon I could see back through the branches to the roof of Tansy House and the fields beyond. Only a month before, I had had to climb higher to see over the wood to the view which stretched across the Border country almost into England. My path climbed between gorse bushes until I crested a rise and walked onto a field of stubble. A figure in the distance was accompanied by two dots, but one of them broke away and came racing towards me.

Boss arrived at a gallop, nearly bowling me over, and fussed around me, panting and sniffing, wanting to know where I'd been and whether I'd betrayed him by fondling some other dog. I had inherited Tansy House from an uncle whose sister had married a southerner and brought me up to believe that civilisation ended somewhere in Hertfordshire. Before putting the house on the market, I had decided to look at it. My uncle's Labrador had been ownerless and would have been put down if I had not taken him in. Alice, who had been my uncle's housekeeper ever since she left school, had also been homeless. It made me shudder now to think how nearly I had turned them both away. But Alice had brought me under her spell, lending a roseate glow to the area where my mother had once had her roots. And now I had put down new roots of my own.

9

Boss accepted my apple-core as a peace-offering and clung possessively to my heel as I walked to meet Keith. Keith's spaniel came halfway to meet me.

Keith Calder was about ten years older than I, but he had undeniably worn better. For one thing, he still had all his hair although it was touched with grey, and there was an athletic spring to his step which was lacking from mine. He had kept most of his good looks, and what time had stolen away it had replaced with an air of distinction at variance with a streak of boyishness which he had never quite outgrown. Ostensibly, he was no more than the local gunsmith and proprietor of the shop catering to those who shot and fished, but in practice he managed to leave most of the retail side to his partner and to deal with the gun repairs in the minimum of time, concentrating his own efforts on matters which he found more interesting and therefore more rewarding.

But Keith was a man of many talents. His expertise, and an easy manner on the witness stand, had led to his frequent engagement as an expert witness, and his quick mind coupled with a penetrating curiosity had often led him to the truth in advance of the police. The consequent trickle of work which this brought him did not wholly explain his regular involvement in criminal investigation. The truth, I think, was that because he was observant, analytical and, having sailed very near the wind in his younger days, well versed in the workings of the criminal mind, he was often the first to realise that a crime had occurred at all. Which made me wonder how often a crime slips by undetected where there is no Keith Calder to poke his nose in.

When Keith had invited me to write up his cases, I had jumped at the chance of a fund of cosy, real-life crime stories which might never sell a million but which would do well in the libraries. I might, I thought, have several years of reasonably remunerative work ahead. In fact, allowing for the need to keep my own pot boiling, it seemed that he was still gaining on me. His adoption of me as a heaven-sent errand boy and leg-man had not helped me to catch up with him.

Keith was carrying a couple of green, canvas dummies. He threw one out and then walked to meet me with his spaniel at heel.

I responded to his friendly greeting with some reserve. I had no objection to being his biographer but I had no wish also to function as his Watson and general gopher.

'What's this help you're looking for on Friday?' I asked.

He smiled at me. 'You couldn't get it out of Alice, then? Get on,' he added. The spaniel, which had been nosing at his leg and gazing, liquid-eyed, into his face to remind him of the dropped dummy, raced away.

'I got side-tracked,' I said. 'She has a talent for it. Tell me.'

We started walking back. 'Nothing much,' he said. He stooped to take the dummy from the panting spaniel with a word of praise. 'Just a pleasant day out in the country, free lunch and a small fee. Picking-up.'

'Picking-up' was an expression which I had heard some-where but it took me a few seconds to put it into context. When the penny dropped, I protested immediately. 'But you know I don't approve of shooting,' I said.

'Nobody's asking you to shoot,' he returned blandly.

'It's the same thing.'

'It's not the same thing at all. The shooting will happen whether you're there or not. The picker-up's job is to use his dog to gather up shot birds. Especially runners which might otherwise escape and die miserably. Looking at it that way, it's an errand of mercy.'

The argument seemed specious but I let it go. 'I couldn't do it,' I said. 'I don't know the first thing about it.'

The two dogs had gone ahead. Keith dropped one of his dummies under the gorse and walked on. 'You've got a damned good dog,' he said. 'And an amazingly good relationship with him, considering that you took him over as an adult. You've kept up his basic training.'

'Only because he seemed to enjoy it,' I said.

'Right. He enjoys retrieving dummies as a substitute for the real thing for which he was bred and trained. You've never seen a truly happy and fulfilled dog until you've seen a dog doing the work it was meant for. Let's see you send Boss back. Handle him onto that dummy.'

Showing off Boss's paces hardly counted as capitulation. So I called him back and sent him out. We were a long way from the dummy by now but he trusted my signals. It took him a few seconds to recognise Keith's scent on the dummy instead of mine. Then he picked it without difficulty. He came back at the gallop, sat and pushed the dummy into my hand, grinning all over his silly face.

'There you are,' Keith said. 'No problem. He'll perform even better on the real thing. And I'll be around to keep you straight.'

I was being pushed into a corner. Keith always could be persuasive. 'But why?' I asked plaintively. 'Why do you need me?'

'Because the keeper's been let down. It's damned near impossible to find anyone with a good dog who's free on a Friday at short notice and one picker-up can't serve a line of eight guns which may stretch a quarter-mile. I can see you don't want to do it,' he added.

I thought that I had, for once, won. 'You're right, I don't.'

'But you're out-voted. I want you to do it. Boss wants to get back to work. And I think you'll find that Alice would like you to go.'

The last was a clincher. After years spent, in London, avoiding the matrimonial intentions of a succession of lady-friends, I had fallen for Alice. And Alice, with the convoluted thinking peculiar to women and despite her Presbyterian fixation on respectability, had moved in and shared my life but had so far refused eleven offers of marriage. She would never expect me to pass for a Scot, she said, but when I could pass among them without causing offence or amusement with my alien ways, then she would marry me.

'Oh, I suppose I'll have to,' I said ungraciously. 'If you promise to prevent me making too much of an ass of myself.'

'I'll pick you up at eight,' Keith said. As we descended the hill, with the wind in our faces and the dogs chasing the scent of rabbits, he began to explain the rules, customs and traditions. It all seemed quite simple.

Not even the prospect of wakening with Alice's copper hair spread across the neighbouring pillow had turned me into an eager greeter of the dawn. There was a time when the most alluring commercial on the television showed a girl who came straight from sleep to joyful wakefulness, to the accompaniment of a fanfare. (This was supposed to popularise a certain breakfast cereal but I suspect that it only popularised girls.) If I had been in that role, a long, low grinding sound would have been more apt.

Alice, however, could have played that girl to perfection. She had me up and even breakfasted in good time on the Friday morning. She had trimmed my beard the night before and laid out one of my late uncle's suitable tweed suits and a pair of stout boots, and even found me a shooting stick to sit on. 'You'll find,' she said, 'that for every few minutes of hectic activity you'll have a gey long wait for the beaters to get round.'

So I had time to take Boss for a turn through the wood, and when Keith arrived in his hatchback I was sitting on the stick at the roadside with the dog at my side.

'You look like the Laird of Inversnecky,' he said – approvingly, I think. I learned later that he was quoting from the great Harry Lauder.

13

'I feel like a prat,' I retorted. I had adapted to life in the Scottish Borders on my own terms, an urbanite who happened to live in the country. Wearing tweeds and with a shooting stick, I felt that somebody else must have taken over my body.

Keith opened the hatchback to admit Boss, who leaped lightly in and curled down with the spaniel. The two were old friends. I saw for the first time that Keith's daughter Deborah was occupying the back seat. Usually very neat and trim, she was wearing jeans and a tattered anorak.

'She's a beater,' Keith said.

'No school today?' I asked.

'My leprosy's broken out again,' Deborah said. 'It always does on shooting days. I think it's psychogenic. If it goes to form, I'll have a miraculous remission on Monday.'

Keith slammed down the door. 'I don't approve,' he said. 'But she has all her Highers. She's only marking time. And beaters are also in short supply on weekdays. They'll probably be equal parts young, old and unemployed. Also, the fresh air does her good.'

'The ten quid does me even better,' Deborah said as we got into the car.

Keith drove back through the local town of Newton Lauder and turned south towards the English border. But he turned again off the main road and headed in a generally south-westerly direction.

'Where are we going?' I asked.

'Aikhowe.'

'But,' I said, 'but that's the Earl of Jedburgh's place.'

Keith decided to take me literally. 'I know,' he said.

'Have you got something against earls?' Deborah asked from the back.

I thought about that. I am not particularly leftish, except now and again when I feel that the Establishment has somehow done me down. 'I don't think I know any,' I

14

said at last. 'As far as I'm concerned, he can be an earl if he wants to, but I think the whole concept's a bit dated. I'm damned if I'm tugging my forelock.'

They both laughed. 'You couldn't,' Keith pointed out. And, indeed, I am getting a bit short of forelock for tugging purposes.

'You know what I mean,' I said. 'I don't think I could bring myself to call another man My Lord.'

'You'd probably embarrass the hell out of him if you did,' Keith said. 'He never wanted to be a lord.'

'I call him Your Noble Lordship,' Deborah said, 'but he knows I'm pulling his leg and he turns pink and falls over his feet.'

'What do you call him?' I asked Keith.

'Me? I call him Charlie. I've known him since way back when. Cut down his first gun for him and taught him to shoot it.' Keith glanced round and saw my face. 'Look, don't get uptight about it. This is one of those shoots where you'll probably find that the beaters are better dressed than the Guns. The old Earl, now, in his day fifteen thousand pheasants were turned out and it was all done by the book. Pairs of guns and a loader apiece and lunch off a white tablecloth.

'He was a character, the old Earl, and a grand old man in his way, but he was a bastard to the boy. Charlie was all brains and nerves and not very well coordinated and his dad used to call him all the names in the book in front of guests, or send him insulting messages by the keepers. I was heart-sorry for the boy and I used to take him out as often as I could.'

'Poaching,' Deborah said from the back. Her parents had tried to keep the details of Keith's gaudy past from her, without any great success. Too many people still remembered.

'That's as may be and it's all water under the bridge now,' her father said. 'At least I taught him to shoot to his father's

15

satisfaction. Rather better, in fact. Relationships weren't improved when the boy started wiping his father's eye.

'The old Earl was a canny man but he wasn't as fly as he thought he was. He got caught by one of the first reinsurance scams. Somebody set up a new syndicate at Lloyd's, handed on a lot of policies at reduced premiums and bolted for the Caribbean with a few million in his pocket, leaving the members to cough up huge sums every time some old rust-bucket plunged to her inevitable fate.

'So when the old man finally popped off, Charlie inherited a large and beautiful house, a huge estate, no money and some farm rents which didn't begin to cover the debts.

'Nobody could have blamed him if he'd sold up. But he was determined to hang onto the place where his early years had been made a misery. Folk are funny that way.

'He'd taken a very good science degree at Cambridge and then, probably to stay as far away from the old man as he could, he'd gone on for a business degree at Harvard. When he came back, the one thing the old man didn't grudge him was money to pursue his scientific interests. Earlier, two small farms had been rolled together into a more economic unit and the Home Farm buildings were empty, so he'd fitted up a pretty good laboratory.

'Young Charlie took his seat in the House of Lords, of course, and using his connections he promoted himself a few minor consultancies, probably with firms who wanted no more from him than his name on the letterhead. But he turned out to be good. Small firms with good ideas could come to him and he'd put the ideas into marketable form. He took one or two other scientists as partners and a young lawyer who specialised in international patent law. They got government funding. After all, they were doing a vital

16

job, helping British high-tech to stay in this country, where it could maintain jobs and earn foreign currency, instead of getting milked abroad or dying of apathy and lack of support. They even have overseas clients now, using the expertise on patents.

'They interact a lot with the universities, but of course a lot of money has to get ploughed into expanding their own laboratories.

'I'm telling you all this,' Keith went on, 'for no particular reason except to explain the financial setup. When the last of those insurance policies expires, young Charlie will be doing all right thank you. Meantime, he has to count the pennies. Last year, he released five hundred birds. This time around, I think he's up to a thousand. The old keeper's semi-retired but still works half-time with a couple of the farm-lads helping him out occasionally. The whole thing's a shadow of its former glory. Charlie just keeps it going for about six shoots a year, for fun, as a memorial to his ancestors and because it gets him some worthwhile return invitations.'

'We won't be overworked, then,' I suggested.

Keith humphed. 'Fifty birds would make a Big Day,' he said. 'All the same, it's a connection I value.'

I was relieved. My mental picture, fostered by television plays which I now know to be travesties, had been of birds raining out of the sky and runners scooting off in all directions while Boss and I made idiots of ourselves under the noses of tweedy aristocrats.

'Is there a countess?' I asked.

'Not yet.'

'He'd make a good husband for Deborah.'

'Don't think she hasn't thought of it.'

'Really! You two!' Deborah said. 'I never thought any such thing. Mum did, though.' She did not sound displeased.

'What does Charlie think about it?' I asked.

17

'He's waiting for her to grow up before he considers the matter,' Keith said with his tongue firmly in his cheek.

Any suggestion that she was still a child was anathema to Deborah but she kept her temper. 'In point of fact,' she said loftily, 'the shoe's on the other foot. His Noble Lordship can be very immature at times.'

TWO

At Aikhowe, Keith brought the car to rest among a group of vehicles which clustered around what seemed to be a former stable block. The house loomed large in the background. It had a certain charm but I could not go along with Keith's description of it as 'beautiful'. Architecturally, it had set out to be a Georgian mansion and had then been embellished with most of the worst features of a Scottish town hall. The gardens, on the other hand, redeemed it. They were slightly unkempt but none the less lovely for that, and were presided over by some towering specimen trees which must have been a century old.

The beaters, as Keith had said, were composed of the old and the young and the jobless, but they seemed a cheery bunch. They all knew Keith and clearly Deborah was a favourite with them. I was introduced around. Most of them had dogs, spaniels predominating, and Boss exchanged courtesies with them. I could sense his expectations kindling. Until then, I had been a great disappointment to him.

The keeper was Mr Macrae and he was never referred to or addressed otherwise. He was an elderly man but tall and still vigorous. While the beaters were climbing into a large pickup, he gave Keith a few words of briefing and a map marked with what seemed to be the plan for a major battle before climbing into the front of the pickup. But he paused before driving off. 'The Laird wants a word wi' you,' he said.

Keith sketched a salute and the pickup moved away. He scanned the map quickly. 'That's good,' he said. 'We can take the car to most of the stands. Stuff the dogs back inside and we'll get moving.'

The countryside was undulating, small woods alternating with fields and hedgerows. Keith seemed to know his way around the narrow roads and soon brought us to where several cars were parked on the verge. The cars were on average larger than the beaters' cars but no cleaner or less rusty. The half-dozen men readying themselves looked very ordinary. There was a slightly higher preponderance of green wellies over black than there had been among the beaters and, before being reduced to a similar state by thorns and barbed wire, their clothes had come from better shops, but I could see what Keith meant. In my uncle's waxed-cotton coat and flat cap, fraud that I was, I probably looked the part better than any of them. Meeting them at the roadside I would have taken them for poachers or worse until hearing them speak. Apart from one man whose accent belonged in an overdrawn film about Rabbie Burns, their voices sounded foreign and yet familiar until I heard myself speak and realised that one and all their voices sounded very much like mine. This, I decided, must be His Lordship's No. 2 guest list or lower.

The Earl turned out to be a harassed-looking man of about my own age but stockier and with curly brown hair and a prominent nose. He broke off an earnest discussion with the one man whose dapperness set him apart from the shooting party and pounced on Keith immediately, pausing to give my hand a quick shake in passing and to thank me for turning up.

'Beautiful dog!' he said absently. 'Yours?'

'I like to think so,' I said. 'But I'll have to watch him here. He's a fanatic. He'll follow any man who's carrying a gun.'

We moved aside to let the dapper man get into the only clean car. 'Typical!' Lord Jedburgh said. 'Keith, I'm glad you're here. We're two guests short. They ran out of road near Scotch Corner and God knows when they'll get here if at all, or in what shape. You have a gun with you?'

Keith only nodded. He always has a gun with him.

'Then you'd better draw a number and we can spread out a bit. Unless your friend . . . ?'

It took a second or two before I realised that he was referring to me. The idea that Lord Jedburgh would invite me to join his shooting party was too outrageous. 'Thank you,' I said, 'but definitely no. And I'm not sure that I can manage the picking-up on my own.'

Keith stepped in quickly to save me from having to admit that I had never done the job before. 'I'll try to look after my end of the guns,' he said. 'If we can't manage between us, we'll pull Deborah out of the beating line after the first drive and she can help you out. Charlie, you could ask the guests to mark their birds down, gather up anything easy and let Simon or myself know what else is to be picked.'

'That sounds perfect,' the Earl said. He and Keith joined the other men, leaving me in limbo until Mr Macrae arrived in the pickup and joined me.

'Are they only just drawing their numbers?' he said. 'The beaters will be started in a minute. Ah weel, it'll no' be my fault if the birds a' gang o'er vacant pegs. Will Mr Calder be shooting?'

'That seems to be the general idea,' I said. 'He says he'll do the picking-up at his end of the line.'

Mr Macrae stooped to scratch behind Boss's ear. From the dog's reaction he seemed to know the exact place where a scratch would be appreciated. 'That'll be fine,' he said. 'I'll watch behind him.'

The group was breaking up. Mr Macrae hurried to have a final word with the Earl and Keith rejoined me. 'That's good,' he said. 'I've drawn six, so you look after the low numbers. If you place yourself in the middle of that pasture . . . ' He spent a few seconds explaining the geography.

21

So I found myself sitting on a shooting stick in the middle of a field wondering what on earth happened next. The calm, universal confidence of everybody else that I would manage perfectly well gave me less than no comfort.

I need not have faced the task with quite so much trepidation. Keith had briefed me adequately. Alice, who was versed in country ways and wanted me to acquit myself well, had read me a two-hour lecture. And Boss knew the job better than any of us.

I heard the beaters approaching, sticks tapping, the occasional call to a dog. Pheasants began to flush from well back, clearing the foremost trees and coming high over the guns. Despite my prejudices, I felt my pulse quicken. Shots sounded over an interval of several minutes but surprisingly few birds came down and those were close to the line of guns. Other birds flew or glided on over my head to the sanctuary of some rough ground far behind me. The beaters began to show among the trees and a whistle sounded.

Boss was looking at me expectantly. 'Go on and do it, then,' I said, 'whatever it is.' He turned and raced away across the grass, returning in a minute with a hen pheasant, stone dead. He sat and gave it into my hand and looked at me again. 'Get on,' I said.

This time he went out to the side and scurried along the hedgerow, snuffling. Mr Macrae walked over as Boss came back with a struggling bird, a cock this time. The keeper took the bird and despatched it with an easy flick of the wrists. 'Twa braw retrieves,' he said. 'Yon's a grand dog you've got there.'

I tried not to swell visibly with pride.

Apparently the beating line was rather sparse. It was decided to leave Deborah to beat. I was to pick up for half the line while Keith, backed by Mr Macrae, looked after the other half.

And so it went on. After the second drive, Boss brought me a bird still kicking and Mr Macrae was not there to help me. Stomach heaving, I managed to wring its neck without pulling its head quite off.

After the third, one of the Guns insisted that a bird at which he had shot was a runner although Boss was showing no interest in the area. Keith had warned me that 'There's always some optimist who's sure that every bird he shot at was pricked.' Looking at the two of them I decided that Boss was probably the wiser. I thanked the Gun and made a token search in that direction until he was out of sight.

As we regrouped at the cars I gathered from the general chitchat that the birds were sparse but 'good'. The last was a comment not on their physical condition but on their height and speed. Gaining confidence I even handed out, patronisingly, some of Keith's pearls of wisdom as my own, to a Gun who grumbled that he 'couldn't catch up with the bastards.'

It was on the fourth drive, the last before lunch, that everything went wrong.

I was beginning to enjoy myself. The sun had come out and there was some warmth despite the brisk breeze. The landscape was as fine as any which I had ever seen. It looked wholly natural, but as I began to appreciate the finer points of driving game I realised that it must have been laid out by the Earl's father or grandfather for the sake of such days as this.

Working the dog behind the Guns was in a sense the errand of mercy which Keith had described. Nor did I find the shooting as offensive as I had expected. There seemed to be no pleasure taken in the act of killing. I could understand, if not wholly approve of, the urge to pursue meat – the urge which, together with a purely masculine love of firearms, impels men to spend so much more money and energy than the meat recovered is worth. It was a pleasant and sociable day spent in the open, matching skills against a worthy quarry which, three times out of four, was elusive enough to hold its own.

The beaters were coming through an area of rough ground, a plantation of very young trees on a steep hilltop. They were still distant, but I could pick out Deborah's slim figure. A cock pheasant rose almost from under her feet and came forward, heading high over the gap between two of the Guns. For a moment I thought that he would escape unsaluted, but then one of the Guns fired. A feather was left hanging in the air and the cock swerved and put on a spurt, climbing slightly to clear the rise on which I was standing. As he went over, I saw that he had a leg down.

No shots were sounding. I turned and watched the bird make for a wood a third of a mile behind me. It was undoubtedly hit and it was well away from the drive. Boss was watching me expectantly. I sent him after it and then concentrated on the action, trying to mark where the dead birds fell and to judge whether those which flew on had been hit or missed.

The beaters came on. There was a last flurry of action and then the drive was over. I looked down. Boss was not back yet. I walked forward to make sure that there were no runners to claim our attention but was told that all the birds had been picked. I returned to my position.

There was still no sign of Boss. And the wood where he had vanished bordered a road which, if not major, was certainly not one of the estate's narrow, tarmac lanes.

Keith approached over the stubble, his sleeved gun slung over his shoulder and two birds in his hand. Herbert, his spaniel, was frisking, evidently very pleased with himself.

'I sent Boss down to that wood and he hasn't come back,' I said.

'He's probably spotted his bird stuck in a treetop,' Keith said. 'You go on down and gather him up. I'll get the car and collect the pair of you. You lunch with the beaters where we met them first. I'm invited to eat with the guests. Enjoy your sausage roll while I dig into the smoked salmon.'

We parted company. I found a gate through the fence which reinforced the nearer hedge and crossed a ploughed field to the wood. I whistled and called but there was no sign of the dog.

Keith stopped in the road and I jumped the ditch to meet him. He wound down a window. 'No luck?' he said.

'Not a sign.'

'If his bird was a runner, he may have followed it far enough. Sometimes a pricked bird goes down a rabbit-hole and the dog settles down to wait. He'll fetch up here eventually. What do you want to do?'

'I'll stay here,' I said.

'Probably the best thing. I'll explain where you are. When Boss casts up, make for the big house.' He pointed along the road. 'The main driveway's about half a mile that way.'

'Thanks,' I said.

He drove off, leaving me very much alone and a prey to worries. Boss might have been stolen. We had a good relationship, but he had already changed owners once. And, like most Labradors, he was a gut-oriented dog. He might have gone with anybody who cared to offer him food. Which reminded me that I was hungry and getting cold.

Still calling and whistling, I began to walk the road, looking in the ditches in case he had been hit by a passing car. I remembered hearing the sound of some slight traffic on the road.

I was just returning to the wood when the same small Ford, cleaner than the average run of cars around the estate, arrived and pulled up beside me. The dapper young man, very dark-haired and with a black moustache, who had been talking with Lord Jedburgh before the first drive began, got out. He was dressed for town rather than country in a well-tailored suit and with just the right amount of cuff showing. Among the Guns, he had stood out like a cock pheasant among crows.

'Mr Parbitter? I'm Donald Lucas. We almost met earlier. No sign of your dog yet?'

'I'm afraid not,' I said.

'Lord Jedburgh says to hang on here until the dog turns up. Unless you'd like to take my car and go for lunch? I could stand guard.' The words were friendly and yet I sensed a reserve in his manner.

'I'd rather be here,' I said. 'Just in case. Thanks all the same.'

'I'm quite used to handling dogs. I breed Dobermanns.'

It was a kind offer, but I could see him turning up with the wrong Labrador. 'I'll stick it out,' I said.

'Can't say I blame you.' His manner became almost human. 'Don't worry, he's probably scented a bitch five miles away. It's amazing how they manage it.' He gave a pat to the handkerchief in his breast pocket. 'He'll show up when all passion's spent. Or when he realises that her owners are too careful for him.'

He left me to it. Thinking that breeding Dobermanns was the last occupation which I would have associated with him, I resumed my search along the roadside in the opposite direction. But there was no shining, black carcass in either ditch.

Twenty anxious minutes later, the pickup stopped and Mr Macrae put his head out. 'Nae sign o' the bugger?'

I shook my head.

'They aye come back in the end. You just bide here, we'll get by. If he's still gone in mid-afternoon, I'll hae the Laird abandon the last drive. The beaters can dae a sweep o' the country, just to see whether . . . maybe . . . he's caught in a snare,' Mr Macrae said reluctantly. 'I brought you a piece,' he added. He handed me out a tin of beer and a small parcel wrapped in newspaper and drove off quickly before I could thank him.

The parcel contained two hot sausage rolls. Although I was hungry, worry had ruined my appetite; but I ate them anyway to pass the time.

Keith turned up a little later. 'I come bearing rich gifts,' he said, 'and insulting messages. No luck yet?'

'None,' I said sadly.

The rich gifts were smoked salmon sandwiches and a flask of coffee, courtesy of his lordship. The only insulting message was from Deborah, asking whether Boss had gone in pursuit of a passing aeroplane, mistaking it for a pricked bird. I am usually shy of teenage girls but I had come to know Deborah well and I guessed that she was trying to divert my anxiety and to conceal her own.

'The missing guests have turned up,' Keith said. 'Battered but unbowed. So I'm relegated to picker-up again. Which means that we can get by without you for the moment. But there's been a theft from one of the guests' cars so it looks like being a late start. You may still catch us before the next drive. Boss didn't have a collar on, did he?'

'No. You said to take it off.'

'That's good. Sometimes a collar can get caught up in cover, or on a fence. I'll have to go now,' he said. 'I'll look back as often as I can.' He hesitated. 'Boss doesn't show any interest in sheep, does he?'

'None at all,' I said. 'I don't think he believes in them. My late uncle seems to have convinced him that sheep are only a figment of his imagination.'

'That's a relief.'

He drove away, leaving me with a new worry. Boss was a gentle dog and harmless around sheep, but I had been told that even a Labrador could be led into wicked ways by other dogs. If Boss had been shot by some farmer for chasing sheep, Alice would never forgive me. I would never forgive myself.

Soon I could hear the sound of distant shooting. Allowing for the same ratio of hits to misses continuing, I guessed that Lord Jedburgh would have his fifty birds.

Keith managed to visit me twice during the afternoon, once between drives and later to say that the beaters were setting off on their sweep of the countryside and that several of the guests had stayed on to join them. Later still, as the light began to fade, I saw a long line of figures crossing the fields. Two or three of them waved to me and I raised my uncle's cap in a grateful salute.

It was dark, but with a full moon rising, when Keith came back again. Another and larger car had followed him and parked a few yards off.

'The beaters found no sign of him,' Keith said. 'As you probably guessed. Are you giving up yet?'

'I can't,' I said.

He nodded, approvingly. 'I thought not. Would you like me to stay with you?'

'Thanks,' I said, 'but there's no point both of us suffering.'

'I thought you might say that. I'm leaving you my car. So at least you'll have somewhere warm and dry to sit. The Duke of Dunbar goes our way, he's going to drop us off. And Charlie gave me ten quid for you and a brace of pheasants. They're in the back. Don't let Boss gobble them. Charlie said he'd have come down himself but he's got enough on his plate. A brand-new Purdey was pinched out of one of the cars and the owner's gone into shock.'

He drove his car off the road and through a gate into a grassy field. 'If . . . when he turns up, drive home and give me a call in the morning,' he said. 'We'll let the local police know on the way by, just in case somebody brings him in, and I'll phone Alice. Otherwise she'll think that we're still whooping it up somewhere. Oh, and Dunbar thanks you for the coaching. He says it definitely helped.'

He collected his gear and got into the other car. As the courtesy light came on, I saw Deborah in the back. I also recognised the driver. It seemed that I had been telling a very scruffy duke how to place his big feet.

The evening wore away. A few cars went by. Mr Macrae stopped with a further supply of beer and sausage rolls, apparently the staple diet for beaters, and kept me company for half an hour, regaling me with scurrilous stories about the nobility in the old Earl's day. Lady Chatterley, it seemed, had been by no means unique. He avoided the subject of dogs. About Sir Philip Somebody who had left one of a pair of new Purdeys in the back of an unlocked car, he was scathing. The shooting community, I gathered, could do without members who were careless enough to invite the attention of restrictive legislators.

We had nothing whatever in common except for an enjoyment of talk, yet I liked the old boy. When he left, solitude and boredom and anxiety set in again. The radio in Keith's car helped the anxious hours to pass but, as night advanced, station after station went off the air.

Some time in the small hours I was doing my patrol, whistling for my dog. I also shouted. A whistle carries further than a shout; but my silver whistle was of the 'silent' type and, despite Boss's instant responses, I was never quite convinced that any sound was coming out of it. I was near the road and I heard a car coming. Something about the rattle of its tappets and the hesitancy of its driver seemed familiar and I stepped out into the lights. The car slowed and stalled and Alice got out of her red Mini and threw herself at me.

'Oh, Simon!' she said. She was near to tears. Alice is an emotional girl, lifted to the stars by some trivial gift and set down in the dumps by a careless word.

'Yes.' It seemed a less than adequate reply, so I went on. 'Let's get your car off the road.'

'All right. I brought you something to eat.'

29

I nearly said that so had everybody else but I had been learning to restrain my tongue. 'We'll share it,' I said.

We parked her car beside the other. Keith's was the more spacious so we got into the back of it. Alice had brought an immense supply of sandwiches and flasks of soup and coffee. Sharing the food, I found myself watching Alice's hands in the moonlight to ensure that she was not sneaking fattening morsels to Boss. Labradors get fat so easily. But, of course, Boss was not there.

It must have been after four and the night was very cold when I got out of the car for the umpteenth time. Alice came with me. She had known Boss from a pup and, anyway, a woman's voice carries further than a man's.

Before we could even begin our patrol, we saw the lights of a car slowing on the road. It stopped beyond the corner of the wood. A door slammed and then there was silence.

'Probably a late drinker stopped for a pee,' I said and, putting him out of my mind, I blew forcefully into the silent whistle.

I was about to add my voice to the summons when the incredible, the unhoped-for, happened. A black shape came tearing out of the wood. I thought that it must be a trick of the uncertain moonlight but it came on and suddenly Boss was beside us. He sat and presented me with a cold and stiff pheasant.

Alice was down on her knees with her arms around him, an attention which he usually considered to be beneath his considerable dignity; but from the rasp of his tail on the frosty grass I gathered that he was enjoying it for once.

'There's a lead on him,' Alice said.

Somebody was coming through the wood, trying to hurry but stumbling over the rough ground in the darkness. I wondered whether he might not be somebody who had found Boss and been in the act of bringing him to me.

30

After hours in near darkness my night vision was well established and I could make out the pale blob of a face nearing the edge of the wood. Aiming to help, I reached in through the door of Keith's car and switched on the lights. Only the sidelights came on, making Alice's red Mini flame scarlet in the night. But when I turned the ignition key there was a sudden blaze of headlamps.

The preliminary glow had given warning and the newcomer had already turned and was ploughing his way back through the undergrowth.

'Hang on to him,' I told Alice, and I ran for the corner of the wood. But I skidded on a patch of mud – I hoped desperately that it was mud – and fell full-length. The other man, once he was clear of the brambles at the edge of the wood, had a clear run where the deep shade had prevented any growth. When I reached the road, his car was no more than a vanishing glow in the distance.

I limped back, brushing off myself the traces of what turned out to be mud. 'How very odd!' I said.

'Weird!' said Alice. 'But we've got him back. That's all that matters.'

'I suppose so,' I said. I bent down. 'Where have you been?' I asked him.

But, of course, he could not tell me. He backed away, wagging his tail with such violence that he nearly overturned himself.

THREE

The Japanese jeep which was the Calders' second car brought Keith's whole family over to collect the hatchback that afternoon.

Even if there had not been an intriguing mystery to discuss, no group as gregarious as the Calders nor a hostess as sociable as Alice would have allowed the occasion to slip away. Over tea and toasted buns around an open fire, guesses were batted to and fro about Boss's mysterious disappearance and return. I must confess that I contributed little to the discussion. Between somnolence arising from inadequate sleep and the distraction of having two lovely women and a nubile teenager in my house at the same time, I could hardly concentrate on a happening which, now that it was over, seemed remote and immaterial.

'If it wasn't for the lead,' Molly said, 'I could believe that he'd gone after a pricked bird. Sometimes they land in a treetop and fall down later, dead.' Keith's wife was small and dark, her looks enhanced rather than marred by the faint scar which ran down one side of her face. Deborah, who was on the way to becoming a beauty, was the image of her.

'That could have happened,' Deborah said. 'And then somebody found him and was bringing him back. But I can't see why he'd take fright and run off?'

'I can see how he might,' Alice said. 'Suppose that one of the beaters was a poacher on the side. He came on Boss, decided to bring him back but didn't want to be seen where he'd no business to be and with blood and feathers on him.' She suppressed a yawn. We had not had long for sleep and in the letdown after all the emotion it had seemed important to make love. And now the flickering of the firelight was adding its hypnotic spell.

'That still doesn't quite add up,' said Keith. 'Why would he follow him up? Let's have a look at the lead.'

'He could have wanted to be sure that Simon was still there,' Alice said. 'I'll tell you something else which was odd. He'd been fed.'

'You're sure?'

'Certain. He'd missed his dinner. You'd expect him to be ravenous. But I fed him when we got here and he could only manage half of it. It's the first time in his life he's left a scrap behind.' She leaned out of her chair to give Boss a pat which he acknowledged with a flick of his tail. 'Gut-oriented, aren't you?'

'He'd probably had a lovely guzzle on something simply horrid,' Deborah said. 'A long dead badger, perhaps.'

Alice shook her head. 'When he does something like that,' she said, 'he's always loose next morning; but he's been all right today.' Suddenly, I lost my appetite. I had come to enjoy living in the country, but had never quite accepted the earthiness of its other inhabitants.

Alice fetched the lead. It was an ordinary chain lead with a leather handle at one end and a ring at the other which could be used to form a loop.

Keith examined it carefully. 'Not new,' he said. 'Well worn but well looked after. I'd say that the handle's been treated with saddle soap. Not the kind of thing that a poacher gets up to. More likely a careful sort of mannie who goes over all his leather – briefcase and so on – and includes the dog's lead while he's at it. There are small tooth-marks in the leather. Somebody's had a puppy around. Which doesn't tell us much. Anybody with a dog had a puppy once.' He looked at me. 'It doesn't add up. It's not as simple as Alice is making out. Dogs do get stolen. Usually for breeding, but Boss has no proven track record for throwing champion pups. Sometimes by some idiot or a child who just plain fancies a dog. But in either case, why bring him back? Anybody so irresponsible, he'd just turn the dog loose.'

'What do you think?' I asked Molly.

She came out of one of her calm reveries. 'There's often a simple explanation for something apparently weird,' she said. 'Someone will probably phone up and say, "I'm sorry I didn't have time to stop and explain when I brought your dog back, but I was rushing my wife to hospital." Something like that.'

She was too loyal to say that Keith was continuing the mystery for his own amusement, but the inference was there and Keith knew her too well to miss it. Their eyes met.

'It may be as simple as that,' Keith said. 'Perhaps Molly's right and I'm looking for a deep, dark plot where none exists. But, on the whole, I think not. I think you blew your whistle just as he was taking him out of the car, and Boss jerked the lead out of his hand and took off, grabbing up the pheasant from wherever he'd put it down. I think you should keep an eye on Boss, Simon, just in case. Whatever he wanted him for, it may not be over.'

But for Keith's warning, Boss might well have gone AWOL again.

On the Tuesday, three days after he had given it, I spotted a serious mistake in the plot of a novel on which I was working. My usual remedy is to take a pad and a pencil and to draw charts and diagrams until I am sure who was where when, and what each individual knew at the time. This is the one part of my work for which I am not tied to the word processor.

It happened that the day held some unseasonable warmth. And Alice was using the vacuum cleaner, the noise of which either drives me to distraction or sends me to sleep, depending on my mood. I decided to take a chair out into the walled back garden where my uncle had created and paved a sheltered suntrap between one of the walls and a judiciously planted hedge of mixed shrubs. Throughout spring and summer this was a secret place, always surprising me with some unexpected blossoms. Even now, a late rose was managing to deck the hedge with white blooms and the mahonia still glowed with purple berries, despite the vagaries of the Scottish weather.

As soon as I opened the back door, I noticed that the door in the further garden wall stood slightly open. I hurried down the garden to close and bolt it before the local rabbits could discover that their favourite restaurant had opened again. At the time, I only thought that one of us must have forgotten to shut it.

But rabbits might already have entered and have fled to their usual refuge under the shed as soon as I opened the back door. I knew to my cost what havoc they could create among the flowers and unpicked vegetables. They seemed to have a special fondness for carnations. I rather liked carnations myself. I called Boss out to investigate.

Boss showed no interest in the shed, to my relief. But suddenly he cocked his head and gave a single bark. Then he moved to the door in the wall and began to whine and scrape.

Mindful of Keith's words, I had dropped Boss's lead into my pocket. I slipped it over his head and opened the gate. He went out with a jerk which nearly had me off my feet and pulled hard towards the corner of the wall, nose down and snuffling.

I dragged him back inside, bolted the door again and took him into the house. Alice was still hoovering. I pulled out the plug.

'I was nearly finished,' Alice said plaintively as the droning died away.

'I think somebody's using a silent whistle,' I said. 'And there seems to be a trail of something attractive outside the back gate.'

'You think somebody's after Boss again?'

'I can't think of any other explanation. This may be our chance to clear up the mystery. Keep Boss inside and phone Keith and the police while I go to investigate.'

'All right,' she said. 'Don't do anything ramstam.' Ramstam, I knew, meant rash.

'I won't,' I said. And I meant it. But I did.

Tansy House stood on its own in open farmland, fronting on to a quiet, minor road. I had several neighbours within less than a mile, but none of them really close or in easy vision.

If somebody were trying to whistle Boss to him, I thought that he would be on or near the road for a quick getaway if and when the dog arrived. I peeped cautiously from an upper window. The fields opposite were fenced with wire and were obviously vacant. To my right, the road soon vanished over a hump in the direction of Newton Lauder. But Boss had pulled towards what was now my left and although the roadside was hidden by a high hedge I knew that there was a parking-place within a hundred yards. It was no more than a length of level verge which had drifted into use for casual parking, but it was where I would expect to find my visitor and indeed I thought that I could see through the hedge the glint of chrome in the thin sunshine and the gleam of a blue car. But it could have been a scrap of glass or silver paper and the blue of a discarded fertiliser bag.

Getting into the field, I tore my trousers on some barbed wire. The field was ploughed and wet earth was soon filling my shoes. Alice was going to give me hell, but I wanted a word with the bastard who had cost me most of a night's sleep and scared me almost out of my wits. There were only two creatures in the world about whom I cared – three if I counted myself – and Boss was one of them.

There was, I knew, a small gap in the hedge at the lay-by, probably made by drivers who had been caught short on the road. Although high, the hedge was not perfect cover. I could make out the shape of a car through a myriad small chinks. All the same, I thought that I had reached the gap undetected.

I was wrong.

I had also jumped to the conclusion, against all reason, that the driver would be sitting in the car.

Wrong again.

I began to squeeze through the gap and almost walked onto the end of a pair of shotgun barrels. My heart lurched and anger turned quickly to fear.

The man holding the gun smiled unpleasantly and poked me in the solar plexus with it. 'Stand perfectly still and you may not get hurt,' he said. 'Any sudden movement and I'll separate you from your guts.' His accent, I noticed, was American and seemed to be genuine. He was no more than my height but much more heavily muscled, and he exuded the sort of brash masculinity which always puts my hackles up. The macho image was supported by khaki slacks and a loose, green sweater. Loose clothes, suited to violent action.

'Who's moving?' I said. My voice sounded squeaky. Mr Macrae, I remembered, had been critical of one of the Guns for shooting at too close a range and reducing his birds to pulp. And that had been at ten yards, not ten inches.

'Keep it that way. Tell me,' he said, watching me closely, 'have they found it?'

'Found what?' I asked.

He studied me again and then grunted. 'That's what I wanted to know,' he said. 'Now, you come with me.'

His finger seemed to be crooked dangerously around the trigger. I said the first thing that came into my head. 'You be careful,' I said. 'If you let off an ounce of lead shot from one of those barrels, you won't need what's left of me.'

The thought was badly expressed but it seemed to get through to him. He froze for several seconds and then smiled again. 'Well, well,' he said. He stepped half aside and used the gun to gesture me through the gap, a gesture which nearly cracked the barrels against a limb of a small tree.

His reaction suggested that the gun was not loaded. Another thought followed immediately. I might not recognise a Purdey at a glance, but being around Keith had at least taught me to recognise quality. And somehow I knew that Keith would have drooled over this gun. The colour hardening on a good sidelock obscures the engraving and does not look expensive to the uninformed eye but there is no mistaking the figure and gloss of a top-quality stock. And my perception was sharpened by a recollection of a gun which had been stolen on the day of the shoot.

'Be careful,' I said. 'That's a bloody valuable gun you've got there.'

My words took both of us by surprise. 'Yeah?' he said. 'You're full of ideas.' He looked down.

That seemed to be my chance. I grabbed the barrels and pushed. They resisted and then flew upwards. My first thought had been wrong again. The gun fired. The blast, close to my ear, made my head ring.

The moment of action lasted perhaps a tenth of a second.

Before the gun went off, I had already launched my free hand in a blow, with all my weight behind it, which caught him on the mouth and threw him back against the car. But, at the same moment, he completed a move which he had begun when I first grabbed for the gun. His knee, aimed at my groin, caught me just above the pelvis and put me down on my back against the hedge, showering me with droplets from the overnight rain. He came off the car and kicked at my face. I managed to jerk my head aside and his boot scraped my jaw and seemed nearly to take my ear off.

There was blood around his mouth. The pain of my blow was only then beginning to affect him and I was becoming aware that my hand hurt like hell. For a moment we glared at each other. In his face I saw a fury which was being unleashed as a deliberate act of 'psyching'. In mine, he would have seen a mixture of emotions. Fear, of course, and mystification and impotent, frustrated fury. It was unthinkable to be killed without knowing why. . . .

He backed up against the car again and levelled the gun at me. One barrel was empty, the other held my eyes and my ticket to eternity. I saw him glance around to ensure that nobody could witness the act. And I knew that, once I was gone, Alice and Boss would together be at his mercy. I tried to get a leg under me but my legs were not obeying orders.

I saw his knuckle whiten as he pulled against the trigger. But he was not used to a double-triggered gun and his finger was still on the trigger of the fired barrel. There was no way I could extract myself from the hedge and get to him before he could move his finger. Waiting was by far the worst of it.

There was a new sound in the air. A car had come over the hump beyond the house. Witnesses were approaching. I thought wildly that if he killed me he would have to kill them too. Thank God that Alice had stayed indoors.

He stooped and looked into my face. 'You have too damn many ideas,' he said. 'I haven't finished with you. Next time . . . '

I wanted to tell him to leave my dog alone or I'd kill him before he could get at me, but I was still winded and my voice would not come.

He turned away suddenly, threw the shotgun into the back of his car and himself into the driver's seat. The car was moving before he had slammed the door. I saw that it was a Peugeot.

The oncoming car was Keith's. I managed to pull myself up, still crouched, and to wave. I was muttering the Peugeot's registration to myself, over and over. Keith, who had seen enough, plucked the wrong message out of my signal and stopped his car in the middle of the narrow road. I had meant to tell him to get to hell out of the man's way.

I thought that the other car was going to plough into him. I could have sworn that there was not enough room between Keith's car and the ditch, but he went through without slackening speed. There was a clash of metal and the sound of fragments tinkling in the road and then the blue car was vanishing over the hump. I let myself down again into the grass below the hedge. It seemed as good a place as any other to get over the shakes.

Keith was hurrying towards me and Alice was running from the house with Boss on his lead. They arrived together.

I struggled and got some of my voice back. 'Are the police coming?' I asked.

Alice shook her head tearfully. 'I phoned Keith first and he said not to call them,' she said.

'Because,' said Keith, 'when Alice phoned I'd just had a call from Charlie. He sounded upset. He'd like to see us both, as soon as possible if not sooner. And he said to bring Boss. He said, above all, no police.'

'Are you fit to travel?' Alice asked me. 'You look awful.'

'You should see the other fellow,' I said. It sounded brave. I showed them my fist which was swelling fast.

'I did see the other fellow,' Keith said. 'Much closer than I liked. I don't think my car will be drivable for a while and Molly's away with the jeep. Would Alice lend us her Mini?'

Alice said that no way was she being left behind on her own, just as I said the same and rather more forcibly. The man might come back.

I got shakily to my feet. God, but the day looked beautiful!

FOUR

Keith, I could see, was in a fever to set off. Something more than the damage to his car was disturbing him. But Alice insisted on bathing my scratches, washing the blood out of my beard and stuffing both me and herself into clothes which she considered more suitable for visiting an earl. My bruises seemed to concern her much less than the appropriate garb.

She also insisted that Keith, after he had phoned the garage about his car, rang Molly. This he tried to delegate to me, but I refused. It was not the first car which had been wrecked during one of our adventures and I was tired of being the apologist. While we made ourselves presentable upstairs, I could hear his voice murmuring reassurance into the downstairs phone.

Alice drove. As a concession to my bruises, I sat beside her and Keith and Boss were tangled together in the back. The small car disliked the heavy load and protested at every hill and corner.

'Do you know what Charlie wants us for?' I asked.

'He didn't say and I hope I can't guess,' Keith said. 'He's been giving me evasive answers for the last couple of days.' Something in his voice made me drop the subject in a hurry.

The Earl of Jedburgh must have been watching from a window. A tough-looking security man was on guard at the door but as we ground up to the front of the big house Charlie appeared at the head of the steps and brushed past. He seemed distrait. His greetings were curt, unlike his previously courteous manner.

He met Keith's eye and shook his head. 'Be patient,' he said. He transferred us to a rather worn Range Rover and we were hurrying back down the drive before I was properly settled in my seat.

We seemed to be heading back towards the place where Boss had vanished. As we went, I tried to give him a brief account of the day's events but he only grunted. He pulled up the Range Rover at the corner of the wood.

'Does your dog like bones?' he asked.

It seemed an odd question but I decided to take it seriously. '"Like" is an understatement,' I said. 'He's an addict. He buries them all over the place.'

'Good. Can you get him to dig them up again?'

I looked at Alice. She did most of the fussing with Boss in the house and garden. I looked after walks and training.

'With a little coaxing,' Alice said.

Lord Jedburgh turned to her. 'Then please do me a favour. I think that he may have buried a bone in the wood. Coax him.'

Alice looked surprised but made no comment. With the air of a mother humouring a fractious child, she got down and called Boss. 'Come on, old thing,' she said. 'Where's that smelly old bone then?' She got a short bark for an answer. They went into the wood together.

'Charlie,' Keith said, 'please tell me that this isn't about what I think it is?'

The Earl shrugged in apology. 'Forgive me,' he said, 'but I'd rather not say anything yet. I could still be wrong and, as you've realised, the matter's slightly more confidential than the date of the Second Coming. If my guess is good, I'll tell you all about it. But only because I'll have to.' He looked at me. 'Mr Parbitter, describe the man who attacked you.'

So he had taken in my story. I thought back and realised that I retained a photographic impression of the man. You tend to notice somebody who means to kill you. 'Medium height,' I said. 'Strong build. Short, ginger hair. The same on the backs of his hands. Small ears, sticking out. Prominent brow overhanging blue-grey eyes. Short upper lip and a full-lipped mouth. Khaki slacks and a greenish sweater.' I paused and thought over my description. 'If I've made him sound ugly, then I've misled you. He's not to my taste, but he's a handsome bastard and he knows it. He could be typecast as the heavy in a film drama, seducing the heroine and deserting her in her hour of need.'

'What about his manner?'

'He sounds like an American and I don't think that it was one of those put-on accents,' I said. 'I'd guess that he has absolute confidence in himself and more than enough ruthlessness to go with it.'

He nodded gloomily. 'That's who I was afraid it might be,' he said.

'He'll be fuller-lipped by now,' I said. 'I belted him a good one in the teeth.'

He nodded again. 'That may be useful. What about the shotgun he was carrying?'

'I don't know whether it was a Purdey or not,' I said, 'but it was certainly of high quality. Colour-hardened action.'

'Twelve bore?' Keith asked.

'I expect so,' I said. 'It looked huge at the time.'

'Had he damaged it?'

'Never mind Sir Philip's damn gun,' Lord Jedburgh said. 'I hope somebody runs a car over it. That might teach the old idiot to be more careful. Did the car sound like the one which you heard driving away last night?'

I thought some more. 'Hard to say,' I said. 'Not large, not tuned up, no exhaust leak. It might be the same or it might not. The driving sounded similar, but I don't suppose there'd be much to choose between any two men taking a smallish car away in a hurry. I got the registration number, if that's any help.'

His only answer was a sigh.

Alice and Boss had been away for several minutes. The place seemed less menacing than it had in the moonlight, but I was becoming restless. I was on the point of getting out to check up on them when they emerged from the wood.

Gently and with difficulty, Alice detached Boss from a large marrow-bone and dropped it through the window into the Earl's lap. 'Here you are,' she said. 'Don't gnaw it while Boss is around. He's a gentle dog, but he'd have the throat out of you for that.'

'I'll remember.' He managed to wait until Alice and the dog were inside before setting off back towards Aikhowe in a hurry.

Instead of taking us to the house, he turned off the main drive into one of the estate's side-roads which brought us to a square of buildings which I learned had been Home Farm.

The Earl locked Boss carefully into the Range Rover and led us into the building. It had once surrounded a square courtyard entered through an archway. The original small farmhouse still formed one side of the square and was occupied by one of the security guards. The stone-built barns and sheds which had taken up the remaining sides had been converted into laboratories and, as business grew, the yard had eventually been roofed over to form the substantial machine shop into which the doors under the archway admitted us. The archway itself was now an entrance hall guarded by another security man. The Earl, I noticed, had parked where the guard could watch Boss and the Range Rover.

Three technicians were busy in the machine shop. Through

glass screens in the openings in the original stone walls we could see tiled laboratories and a range of apparatus which seemed to belong in a science fiction epic. Evidently the business of high-tech consultancy had already grown much larger than I had supposed.

A man in a white coat hurried out of one of the labs. The Earl went to meet him, handed over the bone and came back to lead us into a small meeting room. We sat down at a rectangular table which could have seated a dozen.

It was all very mysterious and I said so. And I asked, 'Is my dog in any danger?'

He looked astonished. 'Not that I know of,' he said. 'Not now. Why would you think that?'

'Digging up bones,' I said feebly. 'Research labs. Secrecy. I could only think of poisons or diseases.'

He managed a faint smile. 'Germ warfare? We leave that sort of thing to Porton Down. No, the answer's more mundane and yet rather wacky. Let's wait until we see whether the panic's over.'

Keith sat in glum silence. Charlie transferred his attention to Alice, chatting pleasantly, but we could see that his mind was absent. I had my first chance to gather more than a vague impression of him. His face did not suggest exceptional intelligence, nor, apart from the nose, was it aristocratic. It was just a face, friendly and slightly shy. But its movements were animated and suggested reserves of concentration and a fount of nervous energy. He was only slightly better dressed than he had been on the shoot, and for the country rather than the town.

The man who had taken the marrow-bone joined us. He was much more like my idea of a scientific earl, being delicately thin with a hatchet face and penetrating eyes. He shook his head and showed the Earl a few small pellets. When he dropped them into an ashtray they clinked metallically.

I saw Keith's lips compress. 'That's what you call breaking it gently?' he said.

Lord Jedburgh sighed and closed his eyes for a second. 'You'd better join us, John,' he said. He introduced us. The newcomer was Dr John Prestatyn.

'We'll have to tell them the story,' the Earl said to Keith. 'I'm sure they'll understand that it's in confidence.'

'You needn't, Lord Jedburgh,' I said.

'Please call me Charlie,' he said. 'I don't answer to anything else. And we need to tell you. One, we owe it you. Two, thinking aloud may do some good. Three, you may be able to help. And, four, Keith will want to know the details.

'As Keith probably told you, we're primarily a research organisation. We do some troubleshooting, but most of our business comes from being approached with ideas which we can put into marketable form, patent wherever they need patenting, raise finance if necessary and then interest the most suitable manufacturers. We get a certain amount of government funding for that side of the work, so we must be doing some good.

'Other, more specialised jobs come our way. In particular, we get a steady trickle of work from overseas, for companies wanting us to modify their product for the British or the European market and do the patenting. And when you think about it, that's a hell of a compliment to our discretion. They're trusting us with major commercial secrets.

'This is an age of industrial espionage. The man in the street may not realise the scale of it but, believe me, it's constant and intensive. You see, there's such a hell of a lot of money at stake, in being first or at least in not being pipped at the post. There are firms which specialise in that sort of espionage and you can hire one of them to find out almost anything in the world. I could name one major manufacturing concern who decided to sweep their brand-new building for bugs before they'd even moved into it. They found more than three hundred microphones, apparently from eight different sources. Incredible, but true. That's how bad it's getting. We sweep our buildings twice a week, sometimes more. Although entry is rigidly restricted, we've found bugs more than once.

'But we were lucky until recently. In Britain we have only one big and competent firm of specialists and, because we're more use to them as friends, they've not only left us alone but protected us from the others. This is the one country where there's no law against bugging devices, only against the use of them, and my lads have produced some State of the Art gadgets for that firm which would make your eyes pop. How, for instance, do you like a microphone and transmitter embedded in a rifle bullet? It can be fired into a building from a mile away and it'll go on transmitting for three months, minimum.

'Last summer, the boss-man came to see me here. We'll call him Smith.' Charlie gave a small snort of mirthless laughter. 'I thought he was going to ask for something else out of Mission Impossible – a television camera which can be strapped to a gnat's leg or something. But no. He'd brought the worst sort of news. One of his ablest men had gone bad. A man who you, Simon, just described almost in Smith's own words.

'Smith knew this character as Dave Reece, but he admits that it may not be his real name. Reece was an American, very skilled and resourceful, with a special talent for electronics and quite ruthless. He was paid by results and Smith's opinion was that he would not have stopped at murder if that would have helped to bring his work to a profitable conclusion. Smith prefers a more restrained approach, not on humanitarian grounds but because he can well do without overt scandal or police intervention.

'After being choked off a few times for stepping too far over the boundaries of the law, Reece walked out and set up in business for himself. He wouldn't have clients of his own to start with, so Smith guessed that he would be looking for secrets which he could sell to the highest bidder. And, on the basis of some hints which Reece let drop before the bust-up, Smith's guess was that he'd decided to specialise. In us.

'Smith was right, as it turned out.

'Since then, we've been haunted. Reece had some capital behind him and he didn't mind spending it on bribes. There have been signs that our mail was tampered with and he's certainly done some wiretapping out in the country where we can't take effective steps. He's had his small successes, although until now they haven't been damaging to us.'

Keith leaned forward. 'I thought that any success at all would damage you,' he said.

Charlie managed a thin smile. 'Not necessarily. The odds and ends which he's gathered so far may have enabled some rival firm of the client to cut its losses – not producing a new line which is going to be trumped, for instance – but the client wouldn't necessarily know or care about that. Nothing earth-shaking. In fact, he may not even have covered his expenses. Cash may be running short while he waits for the big one.'

I felt myself jump. 'Shit!' I said. (They looked at me in puzzlement.) 'I beg your pardon. But it just hit me. Capital is running short. When I said that the gun was valuable, I could see his eyes light up. My big mouth, I'm afraid.'

'You couldn't know,' Charlie said. 'In fact, your careless talk may have saved the gun from being sold in some pub and sawn off.

'If his capital really was running short, he may have been all the more desperate to seize his chance to make good.

'Several months ago . . . Keith, this is your part of the story.'

Keith nodded sombrely. 'Earlier this year, I was smitten by inspiration. Just at the moment, I could wish that inspiration had found some other victim, but at the time it was welcome.

'There has always been dissent between the shooting fraternity and the others. Until recently, it was a hangover from the nineteenth century when the excesses of the new rich caused it to be categorised as a rich man's sport. More recently, the main arguments have been ecological.

'The great controversy of the moment is over the use of lead shot. The sale of split lead shot to anglers has already stopped, and the use of lead shot in cartridges is already banned in parts of Denmark. It's been argued that lead shot accounts for only a small percentage of the lead which gets into the environment, but that argument isn't going to stand up for much longer. There seems to be ample evidence that birds, especially waterbirds, pick up the shot and retain it in their crops along with the grit which they use to grind their food. You could hardly think of a more effective way to ensure lead poisoning. Bans on lead shot are on their way through the American legislature.

'In Britain, we've been sitting on the sidelines until now. But there was a recent case of two hundred geese dying on a Scottish loch. It seems that the water level dropped two feet, uncovering the accumulated shot of generations.

'So it seems that we may soon be faced with a ban on lead shot for wildfowling, and that the ban will ultimately extend to all forms of shooting. There will certainly be pressure to that effect, because the anti-shooting bodies see it as a chance to eradicate shooting altogether.'

As Keith got deeper into his subject his worry seemed to recede while his almost fanatical interest in the technicalities of shooting took over. 'It's this way,' he said. 'Steel shot is not a perfect alternative. Being lighter, it's ballistically less satisfactory; unless it's used with skill and restraint it gives rise to more wounding as opposed to clean kills, which, of course, will generate still more pressure against shooting. And steel shot tears hell out of shotgun barrels.

That may matter slightly less in the States, where they use a lot of single-barrel pumps and autos with replaceable chokes, and barrels are now being made which are supposed to stand up to steel shot. But, over there or here, what of the man with a valuable double gun? He can't risk putting steel shot through it at high pressure. Even when barrels can take it, the choke constrictions can't.

'Many of our present cartridges enclose the shot in a polyethylene wad incorporating a shot-cup. That protects the lead shot from abrasion against the barrel wall. But that shot-cup, formed of several thin petals, is far from enough to protect the barrel wall from steel shot.

'I was lying in bed one night, thinking about something completely different, when an idea hit me for a design for a combined wad and shot-cup which would be totally protective and yet would still open to release the shot. And I came to Charlie for help on types of plastic composition and some moulding problems. I needed a plastic which was tough enough to protect the barrel walls and yet soft enough to relieve the pressure on the chokes.'

Lord Jedburgh took up the story again. 'As Keith explained it to me, it seemed that his design answered only part of the problem. What was needed was a shot which was as heavy as lead, non-toxic, soft and no more expensive. I told him that he might get three out of the four. Gold, for instance, would satisfy all the criteria but cost.' He smiled suddenly, but the smile was gone before it was fully developed. 'Keith said that he'd settle for weight, cheapness and non-toxicity. His shot-cup would do the rest.

'We aired the question at one of our weekly round-table discussions and John, who's our metallurgist, put his finger on an answer.'

Dr Prestatyn, who had been staring into space, gave us back his attention. He stirred the pellets in the ashtray with a bony forefinger. 'I did some research recently for the Swedes. It was on quite a different subject, but one of the spin-offs was an alloy which was both heavy and cheap and which formed pellets easily with the use of a shot-tower. We were ethically obliged to consult them, of course, but they proclaimed themselves delighted to supply the basic material or to allow its manufacture under licence. They furnished a stock of the alloy which the Department of the Environment has already examined and accepted as environmentally harmless. Just to be sure, Fordingbridge has been feeding it to a flock of duck, without harmful results.'

Something came into my mind. 'So that's what all the banging has been in your coach-house,' I said to Keith. 'The activity you've been so secretive about.'

Keith nodded. 'I've had a YTS laddie firing the new cartridge through an old Browning. He's put about ten thousand through so far without any measurable wear.'

To me in my innocence the whole project sounded as if it might be one huge yawn. But Alice, who had been brought up among shooting men, had a better idea of the enormous number of cartridges fired in a year. 'Will the ban cover clay pigeon shooting?' she asked.

'Ultimately, it's bound to,' Keith said.

She pursed her lips in a silent whistle. 'If you can make a penny a cartridge . . . '

'My dear,' Keith said, 'if we can make a penny a box we'll be on the biggest earner since the safety pin. But only if we get in first.'

'You can imagine the sort of security that we've had to maintain,' Charlie said. 'A whole string of valuable commercial secrets is wrapped up in it, yet we've had to pursue patents worldwide, obtain promises of governmental approval and also interest manufacturers and distributors. It's meant driving to public callboxes on different exchanges and dictating documents onto tape at the other end. We were posting packages from remote post offices to accommodation addresses until an overseas

contact got a whisper that his mailing had been inter-
cepted.

'The time is long past when words were enough. We've
had to send samples. We weren't prepared to entrust
them to a hired courier – anybody can be bribed or
mugged. You'd hardly believe some of the expedients
we've resorted to.

'This week, we were due to send samples to a very big
manufacturer in Italy. As usual, none of us was free to fly
over with it. But, for once, circumstances had handed us
the answer on a plate. When he was last over here, the
boss-man had admired the Dobermanns which our lawyer
breeds.'

'Donald Lucas,' I said.

'Yes. I sent him to you at lunchtime, didn't I? Well, the
Italian was in the market for another pair of guard dogs,
so he picked the youngsters he wanted and we arranged
that they'd be sent over when Donald had completed their
training.

'We had two separate travelling crates made and booked
their transit on a commercial flight. Donald was to feed
and water them and see the crates loaded just before
takeoff. It's a short flight, so there was no need for food
along the way. And the crates were designed so that any
customs officer could see for himself, through a screen of
very fine mesh, that the crates contained nothing but one
Dobermann each.'

'Plus one bone?' I suggested. Belatedly, I was beginning
to follow the reasoning.

'Exactly,' Charlie said. 'And the dogs were trained that
no way would anybody relieve them of the bones without
a special word of command being given. As an extra pre-
caution, there was a real sample in one bone and a decoy
sample in the other, with a different word of command for
each dog. Would you fancy trying to take a bone away from
a guard dog which had been trained not to give it up?'

Alice, who fears no dog, shrugged, but I shook my head, emphatically.

'We'd arranged for a guard to go with them,' Charlie said, 'just in case. Nobody knew who he was until the last minute, and he didn't know what he was guarding let alone what the words of command might be.

'The Italian was given a code-word to phone through on the safe arrival of the goods. When that word didn't arrive we began to worry, but only slightly. Italians can be very casual about such details.

'The guard had been told to stay off the telephone and his return was held up by a strike of Italian air traffic controllers. He only reported back this morning. All went well on the flight, he said, and the client took delivery of the dogs. He was kept waiting for half an hour and then the client came back looking about as happy as a pregnant nun – the guard's words, not mine – and told him to get back here fast and say that the goods had not – repeat not – arrived safely. Just two plain bones.'

'And you trust the guard?' Keith asked.

Charlie scowled ferociously. 'I don't trust anybody,' he said. 'But I've questioned him and I honestly don't think he's got the imagination to carry off his story if he was bribed to get at the bones. Besides, he didn't have any tooth-marks on him.'

'I think I'm following you,' Alice said. 'But I still don't understand the connection with Boss.'

Charlie half-smiled despite his worries. 'How could you, Mrs Parbitter?' he said. 'You've only had about ten seconds to think about it.'

'Whereas,' Dr Prestatyn said, 'we've been beating our brains out, mildly since the Italian failed to phone us the "goods received" code-word and furiously since the guard reported back.' He stopped and looked at Lord Jedburgh.

'You go on,' Charlie said. 'I don't think I could bring myself to say it aloud. Besides, you did most of the brain-beating.'

The doctor made the faint suggestion of a bow as if acknowledging a compliment which he knew was well deserved. 'It occurred to us to look at the odd events which had happened at around the crucial time. The vanishing and reappearance of your dog, Mr Parbitter, could have been explained away although the presence of a lead around his neck requires an explanation more convoluted than the obvious.'

'Plus the fact that somebody seemed to have fed him,' Alice put in.

'Had they indeed?'

'We wondered about a poacher who found the dog and was bringing it back to Simon,' Alice said. 'He might well have been shy of showing his face. But it seemed unlikely that a poacher would have bothered to feed him.'

The doctor nodded. 'A dog which was stolen and then was brought back in the early morning,' he said. 'To us, a dog suggested Dobermanns, and bones. And a quite outrageous theory began to occur to us. Outrageous, but the only one which satisfied all the known facts.

'Consider this hypothesis. Somebody within this organisation has been "got at". That would be easy enough. Imagine our friend Mr Reece saying, "I can get millions for that little gadget and you're in for ten per cent if you help me." How many could resist?'

His lordship, who had been studying his own fingernails with unmerited interest, looked up suddenly. 'Could you, John?' he asked.

Dr Prestatyn frowned but he took the question seriously. 'I probably could,' he said. 'Because I'm the one person who knew it all anyway. I would not have had to steal anything. I could just have sold what's in my head. And purchasing power has never meant very much to me. Those are the reasons why you can trust me.'

'There are more reasons than those,' Charlie said after an uncomfortable little pause.

'I would hope so,' Prestatyn said. 'But the others are emotional rather than rational reasons. Now to the theory. Envisage this. The one who's been "got at" does not have access to the "goods" nor to enough information to be able to sell the package. But he has access to the bones and he tells Reece to bring two large hambones and meet him at a certain place and time. They'll exchange and the dogs can go on their way enjoying a perfectly good chew on perfectly ordinary bones while Reece tries to sell the prototype components to the competitors of our various clients – or back to us, if we'll pay enough to keep the information out of other hands.'

'Has there been any offer to sell it back?' Keith asked quickly.

Charlie shook his head. 'No. And I don't suppose that there will be, since Mr Parbitter – Simon – suffered a murderous attack. Go on, John.'

'By mischance,' Prestatyn said, 'the time chosen is around noon and the place is the road beside the wood.'

'Risky,' Keith said, 'with a shoot going on nearby.'

'But the shoot wasn't nearby,' Charlie pointed out. 'At its closest, it was quite a long way off and the place would be hidden by the wood.'

'Quite so,' Prestatyn said. 'But by the sort of mischance which could never be foreseen, a pricked bird gets as far as the wood. Our man is just taking out of his car the two bones which should have gone to Italy when a large dog drops a pheasant, erupts from the wood, grabs one of the bones and disappears into the thickest part of the wood again.' He paused and rubbed his chin. 'If it wasn't so damnably serious it would be very funny.'

'We'll laugh about it later,' Charlie said glumly.

'Probably. But very much later. You may recall that I was against any such unconventional mode of transport from the start. From here on, we're even deeper into guesswork. We don't know, for instance, whether Reece was present at that stage or turned up about then, or whether our man took the next steps on his own. But we can guess that he stood over the pheasant with a lead in his hands and, sure enough, the dog came back soon with earth on his paws. And it was into the car and away with him. Because it's a large wood. Only the dog knew where the bone was buried and they didn't know whether he had taken the critical bone or the decoy.

'Early in the morning they came back. By that time, not reckoning on your unusual devotion to your dog, they knew that any sensible man would have given up and gone home, intending to return and look for the dog the next day. But you, Mr Parbitter, were still there and you whistled at the critical moment. The dog jerked the lead out of somebody's hand and ran to you, grabbing up the pheasant along the way.'

'That must have been a time when you were in great danger,' Charlie said. 'As great as when Reece was standing over you near your home. It seems clear that he stole the Purdey. He must surely have considered knocking you off and recovering the dog.'

'I don't see a dog functioning after seeing its master shot,' Keith objected.

'But would Reece know that?' Charlie said. 'Was that why he held his hand? Or because you switched on your lights, Simon, and he could only see that there were two cars and therefore at least two people? For all he knew, we'd rumbled him and the place was crawling with police.'

'The police,' I repeated. 'Are you going to tell them all this?'

Charlie shook his head sadly. 'The police were told that Sir Philip Dunne's Purdey was stolen. And about your dog's vanishing and reappearance. In fact they've been kept fully informed up to that point – and no further. Here we have to draw the line. We simply cannot allow this story to leak. Just imagine what the media would make of it. They're not exactly noted for suppressing a good story just because some individual, or even the national economy, would suffer. Once our reputation for confidentiality goes up the spout, our livelihood goes with it. So also does the contribution we make to the technological strength of this country.'

There was a moment's silence while, somewhere at the back of my mind, martial bands played Elgar's more jingoistic music. Then I asked, 'What are you going to do, then?'

Charlie looked at Keith. 'I'm hoping that you can help,' he said.

Alice was quicker than we were to notice the evasion in a man's words and tone. She spoke first.

'You say that the police have been kept informed,' she said. 'You mentioned Boss and the stolen gun. But there's something else, isn't there?'

Keith sat up suddenly. 'That's right,' he said. 'What else have you told the police that you haven't told us?'

Charlie seemed to be on the point of making denials. Then he suddenly shrugged. 'Donald Lucas,' he said. 'Our patent lawyer.'

'The man who breeds Dobermanns?' I said. 'And who offered to stand in for me at lunchtime?'

'And hasn't been seen since,' said Charlie.

Charlie drove us to the big house for lunch. Dr Prestatyn walked to join us, arriving with a Cairn terrier on a slip-lead. I saw Charlie look sideways at the dog but he said nothing. I transferred Boss back to Alice's Mini.

The house seemed to be in a transitional state between run-down and refurbished; about half the windows had been replaced and painted, sections of roof had been reslated and patches of fresh pointing were evident. Internally, most of the decoration looked fresh and clean. The building housed offices and computers, but Charlie took us into his private flat, through a door at which the decor changed abruptly from the modern and functional to an old-fashioned and faded elegance. A cold buffet was waiting.

Charlie offered us drinks, but it was clear that this was to be no sociable, vinous lunch. While we ate, we discussed.

'The plan was for Donald to leave during the afternoon,' Charlie said. 'You saw him when he caught me before the shoot, to clear up some question about the guard's expenses. He was almost ready to leave when I bumped into him at lunchtime and asked him to go and see you.' He glanced at me. 'The travelling boxes were already in the back of my Granada estate; with a shoot happening that day, we couldn't spare the Range Rover. All he had to do was to feed the dogs and put them in. He was going to Prestwick, picking up the guard on the way. Which he did. Or, at least, somebody met the guard off the train in Glasgow and saw them all onto the plane and presumably that was Donald. We've shown the guard a photograph of him, but he'd been more concerned about his passport and visa and tickets and whether Italy counted as EEC for bringing back his duty-free and so, as he said himself, it could have been any man with a black moustache stuck on.

'Donald lives alone in one of the cottages on this estate. Nobody paid any attention to whether or not he returned that night. Nor would we have worried, except that we had an agreement that he would let loose any of his dogs which were at a suitable stage of training, to roam in places like the machine shop overnight.

'He seems to be in the early stages of an affair with some woman and he might very well have stopped off. But when I wanted my car back the next day I went down to his cottage. There was no sign of him and his remaining dogs were making a racket because they hadn't been fed. I've been feeding them ever since, but I'm not letting those brutes out, not for anything. You see, I don't know the command for "Don't kill", and even if I did they'd probably think that I was joking. So we've been having to manage our security without aid of man's best friend.

'I phoned Prestwick and the dogs had got away on schedule. We've reported Donald's disappearance to the police, of course, but we daren't say anything which would open up the question of industrial espionage so they aren't yet as concerned as we are. Men do go off for a few days, that's their attitude. They've done it themselves, they said. For the moment, they've listed my car as possibly stolen and that's all.'

'They haven't seen any connection between his disappearance and the stolen gun?' Keith asked.

'If they have, they didn't say so.'

'And was he the kind to go overboard for a woman?'

Charlie scowled at Keith as though he had made an indecent suggestion, but the Earl was only frowning in thought. 'Is there a type?' he asked at last. 'I doubt if there's a heterosexual male alive who couldn't lose his head over the right woman. Or the wrong one. Donald, being a romantic, would be more vulnerable than most. If the love of his life said "I'm sending you to Heaven to assassinate God," he'd go. Smiling.'

Alice had finished her lunch and was sipping at a glass of tonic water. 'Why do you suppose the gun was stolen?' she asked.

'At first, we thought just for its value,' Charlie said. 'Sir Philip was out of his skull to leave it on the back seat of an unlocked car – he'd paid the earth for a perfectly matched pair only a few weeks earlier and now one of them's gone missing. But, if Simon's right, Reece didn't realise the value. We wondered whether Donald had heard Simon announcing that his dog would follow anybody who was carrying a gun. It seems likely. Which points yet another finger at Donald. The others within earshot were the guests on the shoot and would have been missed immediately if they'd gone wandering off. Just as likely is that, when they realised that they were going to have to try to recover one of the bones, they thought that they might need a weapon and took advantage of the opportunity.'

'And then I went and revealed its value,' I said.

'Saving it from being sold cheaply and sawn off,' Keith reminded me. 'Even if he never gets it back, Sir Philip owes you a debt for that. If it had been sawn off and used to kill a bank guard, he'd never have forgiven himself. Charlie, would Donald Lucas know enough to be able to sell his knowledge?'

The two scientists exchanged a glance. 'Frankly,' Lord Jedburgh said, 'we don't know.'

'Obviously,' said Dr Prestatyn, 'the patent lawyer had to have most of the details passed across his desk, but Donald isn't a scientist and they wouldn't mean much to him. A patent application has to say enough to protect the process, but it's usually better to avoid superfluous extra details which might only enable some rival applicant to point out the discrepancies which make his product a separate invention. If we knew when he was got at – if he was indeed got at – we'd have a better idea as to when he might have started taking copies of any critical material.' The doctor frowned and gave his terrier a fragment of leftover chicken while he thought about it. 'Our best guess would be that without the samples he wouldn't be worth his weight in dog-meat. But the samples plus the lab reports, which he could certainly have got his hands on, would blow the whole thing open.'

'And we're not protected by patents?' Keith asked.

'In Britain, yes,' Charlie said sadly. 'Elsewhere, not yet. And Britain could still be flooded with imported cartridges to your design. For instance, we were waiting for the American Department of the Interior to approve the shot before we applied for patents there. Fools that we were, we thought that there was greater danger of a leak from the Patent Office than from the Department. That's why we so urgently need some action on your part.'

'If I didn't have more to lose than anybody else, I'd tell you to go and boil your head,' Keith said. 'Where would Reece make for next?'

'Nowhere in Britain,' Prestatyn said firmly. 'We're protected here. And we've already set up some deals in Britain, and he wouldn't know with which companies. The last thing he could risk would be offering the information to a company which has already contracted to buy it. Where would his market be?'

'Not here,' Keith said. 'We're a comparatively small consumer and a lot of our cartridges come in from abroad. The biggest manufacturers are in the States and Italy.'

'First,' Charlie said, 'he'll have to find out whether he's got the real samples or the decoy. He couldn't risk approaching a possible customer and either being shown up for a fraud or conned out of the real thing by being told that it's the decoy.'

'All he's got to do,' Keith said, 'is to open up a cartridge and compare the wad and shot with the samples he's got. When he sees there's not the least resemblance, he'll know that he's scored.'

'Luckily for us, he doesn't have your ingenuity, or your expertise in ammunition,' Charlie said. 'He hasn't thought of that one yet or he wouldn't have tried for the dog again this morning.'

An awful thought hit me. I must have made some sound, because I found that they were staring at me. 'He's done it by now,' I said. 'My big mouth again. When he was pointing the gun at me, I started babbling. I said something damned silly about him having an ounce of lead shot in the gun, and I wouldn't be much help to him if he let the gun go off. I saw him digest the words and get some meaning out of them which was beyond me at the time.'

'You couldn't have known,' Keith said sadly, not for the first time. 'All the same, I wish you'd give us as much inadvertent help as you've given the enemy. He's probably on a plane out by now.'

'From what Smith told me, all his connections are in the States,' Charlie said, 'so that's where he'll probably go. That's where you tell us that a large part of the world's ammunition is made. It's where the legislation is likely to hurt the shooting man first. And it's where we're least protected by patents. That's where he'll go.'

'Unless he already has a customer lined up in Italy or Japan,' Keith said. 'What do you think we should do about it?'

'If I knew that,' Charlie said, 'I'd do it myself. But we desperately need action, you're one of the few people we can trust and you do sometimes recover stolen goods.'

'I sometimes recover stolen guns,' Keith said. He sighed. 'I've sunk half a year of my life and a mountain of borrowed money into this thing, and now it looks as if I'll have to invest more time and money in the hope of preventing it all going down the plug-hole.'

'We'll split the expenses,' Charlie said. 'I was hoping that this business was going to be our big score. It would have got us off our present shoestring footing with enough to spare to finish restoring the house and make a start on the estate. Instead, it looks like destroying us altogether.'

His look was so haggard and his tone so desperate that Keith shrugged off his own worries. 'The worst hasn't happened yet,' he said. 'I'll do my best. You didn't give up when you read your old man's will. Don't give up now. But I wish you could give me a worthwhile starting-point.'

'I think you'll have to use the police,' I said. 'They can be discreet when the occasion calls for it. Don't you have

63

an in with somebody high enough up? The police have the only network which could watch all the airports.'

Charlie sighed. 'That's true,' he said.

Keith jerked upright. 'No it isn't,' he said. 'Come along, you two. There's somebody we've got to see.'

Charlie came with us to the Mini. 'I enjoyed your biography of Alexander Ferguson,' he said suddenly.

Alice drove off before I could find a suitably modest reply.

'I didn't know that I had the nobility among my readers,' I said.

'I didn't know that he was a reading man,' said Keith. 'Apart from binary arithmetic, of course.'

FIVE

Keith, deep in thought, was uncommunicative. We gathered, from sundry grunts and monosyllables, that he wanted to return to Newton Lauder so Alice headed the Mini in that direction. We had already rejoined the main road when a Jaguar, several years old, came up behind us with lights flashing and horn playing a fanfare.

There was a lay-by ahead where the road had been straightened. Alice turned in and stopped. The Jaguar parked ahead of us and the driver walked back. I recognised him from the day of the shoot, an elderly man with a red face and a white moustache who had been one of the better shots. He was overweight and walked with the care of one whose joints have carried too much weight too far over the years.

'Sir Philip Dunne,' Keith said. 'He'll be wanting me. Better let me out. He'll rupture himself if he tries to stoop to talk through the windows.'

Keith was stuck in the back of the Mini. I had to get out to let him up.

Sir Philip shook hands very formally with both of us and raised his checked cap to Alice. His manner was as stiff as his physique. 'Been chasing you all over Scotland,' he said to Keith. 'Followed you to Aikhowe. Wanted you to see what you could do about my gun. And Charlie tells me you've seen it,' he added to me.

'I think so,' I said.

'Was it damaged?'

'Not that I could see. Circumstances didn't permit—'

He turned back to Keith. 'I wanted to ask you to get after it before some bloody vandal saws it off for a bank robbery. Hell, if he brings it back to me I'll give him something cheaper he can chop up instead.'

This seemed a very odd attitude for somebody who, I now seemed to remember, had been chairman of a large corporation. He must have seen my surprise.

'You mustn't take me too literally,' he added. 'But if he's going to saw up a gun, he can saw up something less expensive than my Purdey.'

'I can't argue with that,' Keith said.

Sir Philip unbent a little. It struck me that he had been on course for becoming one of those pleasant old gentlemen whom one meets in modest retirement, models of bonhomie and good works, until years of power had stamped on him an arrogance which only genuine emotion could penetrate. 'I'm desperate about that gun. Waited most of my life to get what I really wanted. There was never the money to spare. Four sons to educate and all that. Then, when they'd all left home, I thought to myself, "What the hell? If I don't do it now, I never will. The boys are doing all right and good guns are a sound investment. By God, I'll treat myself." So I ordered a matched pair of guns, engraved just the way I wanted them, and all in a fitted, leather case. And I had to wait two years for them.'

'A matched pair was a bit of an extravagance, wasn't it?' Keith said. 'You can't get many chances to shoot with two guns and a loader. They must have cost you the best part of forty thousand.'

'Don't remind me,' Sir Philip said sadly. 'But if you want the very best of anything, you have to spend money. I know that the old ways are changing. In the average year, I get one invitation which justifies a pair of guns and sometimes I save up and treat myself to a day's

66

driven pheasants on one of the commercial estates. And you needn't look disapproving,' he added testily to Keith. 'They say that pleasure isn't gauged by the size of the bag. Well, I'd rather have one good day than a dozen poor ones. Between times, if I can get a good bit of pigeon decoying I like to use the pair of guns at that. My gardener comes along as my loader and we both take a pride in doing the thing properly. It's a knack that we've practised together. And now some bastard's gone off with the Number One of the pair and I can hardly bring myself to open the case and see it half empty. People keep pointing out that it was my own damn fault, and I know it, but that only makes it worse. I was on the point of locking the car when somebody distracted my attention and it went out of my mind.'

'The gun was insured?' Keith asked.

'Certainly. I may have been careless but I am not a total idiot. But that's not the point,' Sir Philip said. 'I'm sixty-six and fit enough, but even if my health holds up my three score and ten runs out in four years. I don't want to wait two years for a matching gun and then not have the time or health to use it. I want to make the most of the time I've got.'

Keith drummed his fingers on the roof of the Mini. 'I appreciate that,' he said. 'Are your insurers offering a reward?' For some reason which I did not understand until later, he glanced at me out of the corner of his eye.

'Bugger my insurers,' Sir Philip said. 'Begging your pardon, Mrs Parbitter. When they get around to offering a reward, I'll top it up. And we'll not argue over values. How does five thousand sound?'

'Musical,' Keith said.

'That's settled, then. I'll look forward to hearing from you. Until then, all that I can say is Thank God I didn't part with my old Dicksons.'

Sir Philip nodded, turned and stumped off back to his Jaguar.

We packed ourselves into the Mini again. 'I could get him good money for those Dicksons,' Keith said. He fell silent again.

Keith remained in his reverie until we were almost back to Newton Lauder, but when Alice pulled in to a roadside filling station he spotted a public telephone and made me let him out of the car again. The tank was filled and we were waiting impatiently before he returned.

'Head back the way we came,' he said as he crawled in beside Boss again.

'Why?' I asked. Part of my mind had been sifting and rearranging various ways of expressing what I wanted to write next and I was anxious to get the results onto paper before I forgot them. But Alice did as he said. Somehow, with Keith, one usually complied.

'I've just phoned Jake Paterson.'

I had seen the name somewhere. 'At the television shop?' I suggested.

'It's a bit more than a television shop,' Keith said. 'More of a Mecca for all the electronics buffs for a hundred miles around. Go right here.' We turned off into a minor road which climbed into the hills. 'We needed a special sort of person and Jake would know where to find him. Mr Haddo sounds ideal for tracking down our man.'

'Why?' we both asked.

'You'll see. Take the left fork up ahead.'

Our road climbed suddenly to avoid a gulley filled with treetops and came out onto heather moorland. We arrived at a neat house perched on the crest of a hill. It had never been a farmhouse but gave the impression of being a town house which had got lost somewhere above the farmland where the moors began. The garden was plain grass, the only feature a large and complex aerial. We disembarked and followed Keith up a short path. He rang the doorbell.

A small loudspeaker beside the door came alive. 'Who's there?' asked a voice, half drowned by some background noise.

'Keith Calder,' Keith said. 'Jake Paterson was going to phone you.'

'He phoned,' said the voice. 'Come away in.' The latch clicked and Keith pushed the door open. It closed again of its own accord and we followed the thrum of a vacuum cleaner into a tidy living room.

My first thought was that if this was Mr Haddo he would not be chasing our quarry for very far. He was managing the cleaner nimbly but from a wheelchair.

He finished the last corner and switched the machine off. 'Sorry about that,' he said cheerfully. 'But once I've started I like to finish. My wife works, so the household chores are up to me. I'm William Haddo. Most folk call me Bill.'

Keith introduced himself and us. Bill Haddo indicated chairs and wheeled himself into a position which completed the circle.

'Jake told me that you wanted some help,' he said.

'I hope that he also told you that you can trust me,' Keith said earnestly. 'Because it's a matter so confidential that I can't tell you more than the barest bones of it. If you're in any doubt, refer to Lord Jedburgh.'

Mr Haddo looked him in the eye for a few seconds. 'Tell me what you can,' he said suddenly. 'Then we'll see.'

Keith paused to gather his thoughts. 'It's a matter of industrial espionage,' he said. 'A man – an American – has got away with samples which could betray the results of months of research. If somebody else benefits, I lose my shirt, jobs go abroad and Lord Jedburgh's establishment loses the reputation for confidentiality which is vital to it. If you can't take my word for those facts, I'll have to go and look for someone else.'

69

Haddo gave a thoughtful nod. 'I know about the organisation at Aikhowe,' he said. 'I was in the oil industry until my accident. So I know what you mean. Go on. What do you think I can do to help?'

'We daren't go to the police,' Keith said. 'They might get results, but the media would have the news before we did. We know who we're after. But we don't know where he's going. He could market what he's got almost anywhere in the world although our first guesses would be the USA, Italy, Germany and after that you name it. Possibly the Orient. We need a quick way to ask the maximum number of people for news of him.

'So I asked Jake for the name of somebody with time to spare, if possible a bit of a linguist, and a keen radio ham.'

There was a silence while Haddo thought it over. I looked down at my feet, but in reality I was bowing my head once again at Keith's ingenuity. But I could see snags ahead.

Haddo put my doubts into words. 'By the wording of the licence,' he said, 'a ham is supposed to confine himself to "Remarks about matters of a personal nature in which the licensee or the person with whom he had been in communication has been directly connected." In other words, just chat. Nothing commercial or political. Seeking news of a wanderer could just slip through within the definition, provided that nobody asks about my direct connection. But how do I broadcast for help and still preserve your secrecy?'

'I chewed on that all the way here,' Keith said, frowning. 'And it isn't easy. We need a message that wouldn't excite the interest of any law officer.'

'And yet,' said Alice, 'you've got to make him sound unsympathetic.' We looked at her and she blushed. 'What I mean is, you can't broadcast a request for news of him on the grounds that, say, his old mother's dying, or the

70

first person to see him would say, "Here, they're trying to reach you.'"

'And then the jig would be up,' Haddo said.

'Wouldn't it!' Keith said. 'Suppose we made him a homosexual who'd deserted his boyfriend?'

'There are still some who'd be on his side,' Haddo said carefully. 'Especially in the States. If he's gone to San Francisco . . . '

'Well, even a fairy has a mother,' Keith said. He found an envelope in his pocket, borrowed a pen from me and started to scribble. 'He's deserted his poor old mother, cleaning out their joint account and leaving her penniless. We want news of him without his being warned, so that a process-server can catch up with him. How's that?'

'We can polish it,' Haddo said. 'It stretches "Remarks about matters of a personal nature", but not quite to breaking point.' He looked at his watch. 'Evening and through into the small hours, local time, is when you get most of them listening.' He wheeled himself across the room and opened a cupboard, revealing a compact transceiver with its ancillary equipment. He lowered a flap to form a small desk on which he opened a copy of a magazine. 'I'll put this onto tape and get it around Europe straight away. America will have to wait until the middle of our night, and then the Orient when it's early morning here. That depends on conditions being suitable, of course.' He ran his finger down a page in the magazine. It was headed, 'F-layer Propagation Prediction.'

'You'll have to sleep some time,' Keith said. 'If they can't raise you on the radio they can phone me at home, collect.'

'But what about all the different languages?' I asked.

'No problem,' Haddo said, leaning back in his wheel-chair. 'English is the preferred language. When I make an English-speaking contact, I can ask him to pass it around his own territory. Or I read the message to him. He repeats it back to me in his own language. I tape it. I'm not allowed to replay the tape over the air, so I repeat his translation in my own voice onto another tape and broadcast it as a CQ call. That's a general call to anybody who wants to listen. Simple as that. It's been done before.'

'Simple as that!' I echoed.

He chuckled. 'Well, it is,' he said. 'By the time I've spoken to a hundred people and each of those has spoken to fifty and asked them to pass it on . . . '

'By then, it should have reached somebody who's seen him,' Keith said. 'But whether he bothers to call back is something else again.'

'If he's a ham, he'll call back,' Haddo said. 'They're always dying for an excuse to blether.'

The Calders lived in the country to the north of Newton Lauder in an attractive Victorian house – far more attractive, in my opinion, than Aikhowe although less grandiose. We were, of course, obliged to run Keith back. I offered him drinks at Tansy House, which would have brought me home where I could then have relaxed at leisure while Alice went on with Keith but, uncharacteristically, he declined. He also jibbed at being dropped at the gates when we arrived at Briesland House but persuaded Alice to take him right to the door.

The Calder family always gave such an impression of solidarity, and of a hierarchy with Keith firmly at its head, that I would never have guessed that he felt the need of moral support. He must have sensed Molly's disquiet during his phone call of the morning. We were left in no doubt that she had spent the day imagining Keith's accident but with a variety of less happy outcomes.

Alice made a circle on the gravel and parked outside the front door. Before she had time to pull up the handbrake, Molly's head had arrived at the open window beside me. 'Where have you been all day?' she demanded of Keith. We might not have been there at all.

'I told you we were going to— ' he began.

'Wal's been trying to find you. And what happened to the car?'

'Somebody— '

'It's too bad of you!' she snorted. She was very white about the face. 'And it's not the first time. I suppose you were tearing around as usual, too busy talking to pay attention?'

'I was already stopped,' Keith said loudly. 'Wasn't I?' he added in my direction.

With Molly established in the window, I was unable to move and let Keith out. 'That's quite true,' I said. 'Alice phoned Keith because there was somebody hanging around the house. When he arrived, I'd been attacked. The man drove off and collided with your stationary car.'

'I saw it all,' Alice said quickly. 'That's exactly what happened.'

Molly looked hard at me, saw the graze on my ear and tutted.

'Let me get out and I'll tell you all about it,' Keith said. 'You'll be interested.'

Bending down to a Mini's window is a long stoop. She straightened up while she thought it over, which gave me a chance to open the door and get out of the car. Keith followed me out like an animal escaping from a trap.

'Well, all I can say is that it happens too often,' Molly said hotly. 'If I bust as many plates as you do cars, I'd soon hear about it. You get involved in these violent things and one of these days you're going to get yourself killed and then what about Deborah and me?' Her voice, as she finished, was almost a wail.

Keith put his arms round her. 'This time,' he said, 'I can't keep out of it. Our whole future's at stake.'

73

I got back into the car and made driving-off signals to Alice, but she was spellbound.

'That doesn't justify taking stupid risks,' Molly was saying. 'Maybe you weren't at fault this time, but you do get yourself into the most awful scrapes. We've been broke before and we were happy. Can't you see that we'd rather be broke again than risk being without you? Charlie phoned,' she added without any change of tone. 'He said to call him back but it isn't urgent. Well, you needn't think that you're running all over the place at his beck and call. The jeep's mine until you get the car fixed.'

'But I've got to get in to the shop,' Keith said.

'When did you even care about going to the shop? I'll run you there and fetch you back and that's all.'

She turned back to the house and Keith went with her. I nudged Alice again and we drove off.

'And that goes for you too,' Alice said firmly. I could have asked whether she was referring to transport or to not being ramstam, but the moment seemed inopportune.

Molly phoned an hour later. Alice had gone out, so I took the call. Molly wanted to apologise, she said. She was her old, calm self; indeed, her voice held the warm gentleness of a woman who has been reassured of her partner's love. Keith, it seemed, had expressed himself in the way which came most naturally to him. His example is not one which I would always care to follow, but in this instance he seemed to have hit on the right treatment.

SIX

In the same way that sleep is impossible while you wait for the other shoe to hit the floor, and one cannot absorb heavy reading in the company of someone in the habit of demanding sudden and urgent attention, so I can never settle to work when interruption is in the wind.

Quite sure that I had not heard the last of Keith and his stolen secrets, I found that I was waiting next day for the phone to ring when I should have been concentrating. So when Alice asked whether I wanted to join her in a trip to Newton Lauder, I went along. Anything, even shopping, would be better than sitting at home staring at a blank screen.

Newton Lauder is a small town, pleasantly old-fashioned. Most of it was built during periods when standards of both design and construction were high and it has since been graced with more than its share of trees and gardens. But it does not have much to entertain the casual stroller when a thin drizzle is drifting on the wind, darkening the pavements and driving the girls indoors. Licensing hours had not yet arrived. Having jibbed at accompanying Alice into the one supermarket and after studying the displays in the other shop windows, I was at a loose end.

Sight of the Calders' jeep parked in the Square suggested that Keith might well be in town. If not, at least I could pass the time of day in the warm, dry shop with Wallace James, his partner.

Keith and Wallace were in the otherwise empty shop, arguing without heat over the condition of a gun, well worn but bearing a famous name, which Wallace had taken as a trade-in.

'Send the barrels away for blueing,' Keith said at last. 'I'll sort the rest of it.'

Wallace was nursing a clipboard heavy with lists but Keith turned to me with evident relief. He had an intense loathing of the mundane routines of business life although Wallace, who had begun his professional life as an accountant, seemed to thrive on them.

'I was wondering what Charlie called up about,' I said.

Wallace threw up his eyes and turned away to continue checking stock.

'Nothing earth-shaking,' Keith said. 'His secretary had offered to feed Donald Lucas's dogs once before when Lucas went off. It seems that he phoned up on Friday night to ask her to do it again. Her mother took the message and forgot about it.'

'Mystery resolved,' I said.

'Maybe. The mother had never heard Lucas's voice,' Keith said. 'But Bill Haddo phoned up this morning. He wants to report progress.'

'And I want to g-get these orders away,' Wallace put in.

'You carry on. Whatever you order will be all right with me.'

'And won't you half complain when the time comes to sign the cheques,' Wallace said. His slight, natural stammer is inclined to disappear when something annoys him. 'You've got time to initial the orders.'

'Gimme.' Keith grabbed the clipboard and began to jot his initials without reading anything. 'I'm sorry I got us into this mess, Wal,' he added humbly. 'You were always agin it.'

I realised for the first time what I should have guessed, that the development of the new cartridge was the concern of the business and not Keith's private venture.

Wallace shrugged. 'I was acting as d-devil's advocate. It was a reasonable bet. It still may be. At worst, we're back where we were ten years ago.'

'And Charlie takes a hell of a knock.'

'Lord Jedburgh deserves whatever's coming to him,' Wallace said with some heat. 'He undertook to send the samples out to Italy and he buggered about, if you'll excuse me, Simon, with tenth-rate James Bond gimmicks, hiding the stuff in dogs' bones for God's sake! I'm only surprised he didn't throw in an explosive booby-trap or a poisoned needle.' He paused and smiled reluctantly. 'I'd have g-given an arm and a leg to have been hiding behind a tree when Boss came out of the wood and grabbed it.'

'It has its funny side,' Keith admitted. 'We owe Boss a genuine bone. If he hadn't let greed take over from his training we wouldn't have a starting-point at all.'

Wallace raised one eyebrow at him. 'Looking at it the other way up, if you don't catch up with this man Reece – and I don't rate your chances very highly – B-boss's interference has had us throwing good time and money after bad, so d-don't lash out on any jumbo hambones just yet. You must have been out of your skulls, the lot of you! If you needed a courier, I'd have gone to Italy.'

'But would you have come back?' I asked.

Wallace glanced out of the window at the chill drizzle. 'Not if I could bloody well help it,' he said, flourishing his clipboard. 'Oh, for God's sake! Run along, Keith, and see what Haddo's got. I can hold the fort.'

Keith made his escape and I followed him outside. 'Do you want to come and see Bill Haddo with me?' he asked me.

After a moment's thought, I decided that I was curious. 'Do we have transport?' I asked.

'I have the jeep,' he said. He seemed surprised that I should doubt it.

'I'll join you in a minute,' I told him.

Newton Lauder is not of a size to support a very large supermarket. Alice was easily found, browsing through the frozen food cabinets. I told her where I was going. She hesitated and then nodded.

Keith drove us southward with the radio playing the Bruch Violin Concerto above the buzz and rattle of the small vehicle and the thwack of the wipers. It finished as we climbed towards Bill Haddo's house and Keith turned the radio down. 'I'm not expecting results this early,' he said. 'I just didn't feel up to doing anything else.'

'That's how I feel,' I said.

The tall aerial, I noticed, was rotating under its own power as Haddo homed in on radio traffic. It froze when we rang the bell. The remote gadgetry admitted us. There was a coffee-pot and cups on a low table. Haddo was at his radio desk and he spoke to us from behind a coffee-mug the size of a chamber-pot.

'I've had a dozen possible sightings,' Haddo said. 'It's up to you whether you follow any of them up, but I'd suggest not – the next day or two should sort the wheat from the chaff. This one' – he pushed aside a slip of paper – 'was from an Irishman who is always a close friend of anybody you care to mention.'

Keith looked up from pouring coffee. 'One of those,' he said.

'One of those. Another sounded probable, but the sighting was last Tuesday, mid-morning, in Oslo.'

I shook my head. 'We know where he was then,' I said.

'That's what I thought. And you can't follow up every man with a bruised face, colour of hair not known because he was wearing a hat.'

'How many of those?' Keith asked.

Haddo counted slips. 'Eight,' he said. 'Aberdeen, Toronto, Channel Islands, Dallas, Minorca, Paris and two in Cornwall –

both the same chap, from the sound of it, but the descriptions don't sound much like your man.'

'Most of the places sound unlikely,' Keith said. 'I can't see him rushing to Minorca with industrial secrets.'

'That's what I thought. We're left with one good sighting, but it may be too early to be helpful. Perth, after lunch on Tuesday. My contact was collecting his car from one of those riverside parking places when a blue Peugeot came into the slot beside him. He took notice because the car had been in a front-end accident and he didn't want to be the victim of the next one. The man who got out was wearing a hat, but he had a swollen mouth and the rest of the description tallies. Does that help?'

'It could,' Keith said, frowning. 'Just what the hell he'd be doing in Perth beats me. But it could certainly help.'

The radio receiver began to speak and a second later the phone rang beside me. Haddo turned to the radio and Keith was listening intently, so I picked up the phone. 'Bill Haddo's house,' I said.

'Is that you, Simon?' said Wallace's voice. 'Tell Keith that Lord Jedburgh's been on the phone again. Strathclyde Police rang him. His car's been found, with a body in it. They want him to go over there, straight away, and he wants Keith to go with him and hold his hand. What does he need Keith for?' Wallace demanded indignantly.

'I think that he looks on Keith as his big brother,' I suggested.

'If Keith was his big brother he'd be the Earl,' Wallace pointed out. 'Anyway, I told Lord Jedburgh where to find Keith and I think he's on the way to you now.'

'I'll tell him,' I said.

The radio call had been from some ham wanting to chat about the weather. I relayed Wallace's message to Keith.

'Was there no indication as to whose body?' Keith asked sharply.

79

'That's probably what the police want Charlie to tell them,' I said.

'Of course.' Keith scratched his head. 'If it's Reece's body it could change everything, not necessarily for the better.'

'Shall I suspend my side of it?' Haddo asked.

'Not yet. If it's Reece I'll phone you.'

Haddo nodded. 'You've a long journey ahead of you,' he said. 'If you want the bathroom, it's the last door on the right.'

Bill Haddo's house was no more than fifteen miles from Aikhowe. We soon heard a car slowing at the gate and Keith and I went out to join the Earl.

He was driving Donald Lucas's small Ford and readily agreed to pick Keith up at Briesland House so that the jeep could be returned to Molly. There seemed to be a general assumption that I was going to go with them. I got in beside Charlie rather than ride in the less comfortable jeep.

'This is the best I could borrow at short notice,' Charlie said, following the jeep down the hill. 'The Range Rover's fetching supplies from Edinburgh and my car seems to be stuck on a hilltop near the west coast with a corpse inside. This was still outside Donald's door. If the corpse is Donald's he won't mind and, if it isn't, he owes me the loan of a car. But I shouldn't be making jokes,' he said quickly.

'Either way,' I said, 'it looks very much as if he sold you out.'

'That's true. But he is or was a member of my staff. I feel responsible.'

He continued to beat his breast, metaphorically speaking, until we were at Briesland House. I moved into the back seat. Keith, I noticed, was only in the house for long enough to give Molly the barest minimum of an explanation before hurrying out and taking the front passenger's seat. Charlie set off again.

'Where are we going?' Keith asked absently. Almost as a reflex, he looked through the nearer door pocket and then began a search of the glove compartment.

'One of the small towns inland from Irvine,' Charlie said. 'I've got directions written down. And I had a postcard from Donald this morning.'

'You what?' Keith said.

'Written on Saturday, postmarked in Edinburgh, date of postmark unclear and not delivered for nearly a week. That's the Post Office for you,' Charlie said angrily. 'The card says that he's caught up with his work and he's taking a few days off. He apologises for keeping my car and hopes that I can manage without it for a while.'

'Why would he write to you,' I asked, 'instead of phoning? He phoned your secretary, even if he only got her mother.'

'Because I'd have told him to bring my bloody car back and make do with his own little vehicle. Wanted to cut a dash, I suppose.'

'Your big estate car's better adapted for fornication in the back,' Keith said. 'Was the card in his handwriting?'

'It looks like it, although it would be an easy hand to forge. Very neat and round, almost childish.' Charlie turned off in the direction of Peebles and drove in silence for a few miles through hilly but fertile farmland. The rain was heavier on the high ground and the wind got hold of it, rattling it against the car. 'If he returned as far as Edinburgh,' Charlie said suddenly, 'what was Donald doing back near Prestwick Airport?'

'If it's his body . . . ' Keith said absently. He was examining a scrap of paper from under the passenger's seat. 'Here's one answer. A hotel receipt. It seems that a Mr and Mrs Lucas spent a weekend at the Greenmilns Inn about three weeks ago. That's one of those cosy little country hotels near the west coast, isn't it? Much favoured by honeymooners?'

'If there's a Mrs Lucas,' Charlie said, 'I've never heard of her. Unless it was his mother. But that was the weekend when he asked my secretary to feed the dogs. He must have been on a dirty weekend with the new girlfriend.'

'There's your answer then,' Keith said. 'Either he drove to Edinburgh, collected the lady-love and took her back to the hotel where they'd had such a splendid time three weeks ago; or else he gave her the card to post and she forgot about it until she was back in Edinburgh. Take your pick.'

Charlie was only half listening. 'Keith,' he said suddenly, 'if it is Donald's body, we'll have to tell the whole story, won't we?'

'Probably. Play it off the cuff, take your line from me, say as little as possible and that only after obtaining an oath of secrecy.'

'There's always some damned copper with a friend on the local rag,' Charlie said glumly.

'Cheer up,' Keith said. 'It may be some casual car thief with a dicky heart.'

'Then where's Donald?'

'Continuing his illicit honeymoon and far too busy to look out of the window and see that the car's gone,' Keith said. 'Lucky sod!'

Death and betrayal must have been in both their minds because neither had any appetite for lunch. We arrived well before two at the small town's police station, an ugly building made hideous by painted brickwork. I tried to sneak off for a quick snack while Keith and Charlie went inside, but Keith would have none of it. They might want me, he said, as a witness.

'Witness to what?' I asked.

'To what we said or didn't say. You don't have to listen, we'll tell you later what you heard.'

Inspector Strachan was at his desk and came out to meet us. As Keith said later, he was 'A bland sort of chiel with a notebook instead of a brain and no more social grace than to keep a lord standing in a corridor.'

'Very good of you to come yourself, Lord Jedburgh. Your car's still where we found it but the body is at the hospital, awaiting the pathologist. My sergeant will go with your lordship.' The Inspector was evidently a lover of titles.

'And then do you want me back here?'

'That won't be necessary, my lord.' (Charlie caught Keith's eye.) 'If you can confirm the identity of the body – or otherwise – just tell my sergeant and he'll write out a brief statement for you to sign. You may be called to give evidence of identity if the fiscal decides on an enquiry. But it's as clear a case of suicide as ever I saw. He drove well off the road and ran a hose from the exhaust to the car's window. He seems to have drunk most of a bottle of vodka to give himself courage and then started the engine. It had stopped for lack of fuel by the time they found the car early this morning.' The Inspector paused and shuffled his feet. It seemed to be against his principles to ask pointed questions of an earl. 'Why would he be in your car, my lord?'

'One of his staff had been to Prestwick Airport for Lord Jedburgh,' Keith said. 'That may be who it is.'

'But I don't know of any reason why he'd kill himself,' Charlie said. 'He wasn't depressed when I last saw him.'

'Is that so? But it's not so strange,' said the Inspector. 'The happiest seeming folk sometimes do away with them-selves, my lord. It just takes a sudden change of mood. Too late to change your mind back again after you're gone.'

Keith had been frowning at his friend but his signals were ignored. 'Then there were no suspicious circumstances?' Charlie asked.

The Inspector seemed surprised at the very idea. 'None that we've found so far,' he said. 'The only clear fingerprints to be found were the man's own.'

'Can I collect my car?'

'Now, there I must disoblige your lordship. I've men up there now conducting a search and until the procurator-fiscal has seen the reports of myself and the pathologist I'll have to ask you to leave it in our hands. It will be well treated. Your lordship will understand that we have to take every care in such a case. It would never do if we were to find that we had a case of murder and the evidence scattered to the four winds.' The Inspector smiled faintly, pleased with the breadth of his own imagination.

The Sergeant was lean, dark and socialist – or, at least, he was less inclined to scatter 'lordships'. We followed his blue and white car out to the hospital.

'Do curb your natural desire to blether,' Keith told Charlie. 'There's no need to start anyone thinking, especially one whose mind is obviously blank at the moment, like our friend the Inspector. And don't make statements which can be disproved later. Simon, you did not, repeat not, hear Charlie say anything about not knowing any reason why Donald Lucas should kill himself.'

'Shouldn't I tell them about the postcard?' Charlie asked unhappily.

'You should. But don't. Not yet.'

'What about the hotel receipt?'

'Same answer,' Keith said shortly.

We waited in the car until Charlie came out, looking green. 'It was Donald,' he said. 'I signed a statement.'

The Sergeant nodded. 'If that'll be all, gentlemen . . . ?'

'One moment,' Keith said. 'Lord Jedburgh would like to take a look at his car. Just to reassure himself that it's undamaged.'

Charlie nodded.

'I went round it myself,' the Sergeant said. 'Not a mark on it.'

'I think his lordship has the right to satisfy himself,' Keith persisted. 'There may be marks you missed. You wouldn't want the police to be blamed for them.'

The Sergeant sighed. 'Very well,' he said. 'Follow me again.'

The rain had stopped or else we had driven out of it. We followed the panda car out of the town and along the floor of a broad valley. The road crossed and recrossed a small river which washed the roots of tall trees. The hills above were bare except for grass, with here and there a panel of forestry plantation draped on a hillside as if to dry. The Sergeant led us off the road and into one of the biggest tracts which was cut up into smaller areas by roads and firebreaks as well as by natural gulleys.

'I saw what he had in his pockets,' Charlie said.

'Anything of interest?'

'Damn-all. Just the bare essentials. Nobody ever had pockets so devoid of odds and ends and scraps of paper.'

'His pockets may have been emptied by whoever killed him.'

'Oh, come on!' Charlie said. 'He was the sort of man who empties his pockets every night. Why would anyone kill him?'

'I can think of more than one possible motive.'

'And I can think of three very good motives for suicide. One, remorse. Two, Reece bilked him of his share. Three, the lady-love broke it to him that she'd only been leading him on.'

'And if you think about it,' Keith said, 'each of those could be an equally good motive for murder.'

Charlie thought about it and grunted unhappily.

We followed upward by ways which deteriorated until we were crawling along ruts and scraping the silencer on the hump between.

The Sergeant parked at last on an area of stony ground, got out of his car and beckoned. We joined him. It was a cheerless place. If I were ever to contemplate suicide, I would want my last sight of earth to be of flowers and grass, not sodden conifers. Even without the drizzle, it was damp and cold. Keith had on his winter sheepskin, I had my uncle's old, waxed cotton waterproof but Charlie, in a thin coat, was shivering.

The Granada was tucked almost out of sight among the conifers. The driver's window was slightly open. A length of polythene pipe trailed across the bare ground. A bored-looking constable was peering dismally at the surface of a neighbouring firebreak and I could hear faint sounds of activity from among the trees.

Some garment of wool or, more probably, man-made fibre, lay beside the driver's door. Keith stirred it with his toe. 'How did he take the end of the pipe inside?' he asked.

'Through the driver's window,' said the Sergeant. 'He stuffed the gap with yon old sweater. We'd best gather it up for Forensic.' He added a sound which could have been taken for 'M'lord.' He turned away and called to the visible Constable.

'The inside of the car's a lot tidier than I ever left it,' Charlie said. 'There's nothing to be seen at all. My cars tend to fill up with toffee papers and credit card slips.'

'Maybe the fuzz cleaned it out.'

'The Sergeant only mentioned the vodka bottle,' Charlie said, frowning. 'But I could believe that Donald cleaned it out before collecting his girlfriend. He was that sort of a person. Finicky.'

The Sergeant, having seen to the bagging of the sweater, came back. 'I must away,' he said. 'I'll thank you not to touch the car until we're finished with it. Good day to you, gentlemen.' He turned away and soon they heard his car start and begin to crawl down the track.

'Was Donald Lucas a drinker?' Keith asked softly.

'Never, come to think of it,' Charlie said, 'except for an occasional beer. He had something wrong with his ears and one small sherry just about knocked him flat.'

'If I were topping myself,' Keith said thoughtfully, 'I wouldn't take the hose in through the driver's window where it would be blowing carbon monoxide right into my ear. You noticed the sweater?' he asked me.

'That's the one Reece was wearing when I met him,' I said. 'Or one damn like it.'

'Dear God!' Charlie said. 'I'm cold and my feet are wet. What do we do?'

'We don't bother searching,' Keith said. 'The police aren't giving this the full treatment but they'll already have lifted anything interesting and we don't want to put ideas into their little, pointed heads. I think . . . Yes, I think we go and try to find a friend. At least, he used to be a friend of sorts. And he was flexible enough to bend the rules a bit when they got in his way.'

We found a roadside phone box. Keith went in. I gathered from his expression that the box had been used for purposes not envisaged by its designer, but at least it contained a telephone in working order and, because Keith held the door ajar, I could follow his side of the ensuing discussions from the car.

It took several calls before Keith made contact with Cathcart. His enquiries after Inspector Cathcart met with blank incomprehension, but when he remembered that it was some years since he had last had dealings with the Inspector and began to ask for a chief inspector of that name, one of the succession of operators with whom he had been wrestling suggested that there was in fact a Superintendent Cathcart. Would that be who the caller was wanting?

Keith said that it would.

The Superintendent had not forgotten Keith. He must have opened the discussion by asking what Keith wanted this time.

'A very confidential chat,' Keith said. ' . . . As confidential as you can possibly make it without getting your head in a sling. We could be with you in under an hour.' He listened for a few seconds, then disconnected and came back to the car.

We set off again. 'That,' Keith said, 'is one of the shrewdest bastards on the Force. If he were more of a politician he'd end up as Commissioner of the Met. There's a roadside restaurant just this side of Drumboy and he said to be there in half an hour and not to break any speed limits. In other words, he picked a meeting place almost exactly halfway between us. He meant me to know that he knew precisely where we were. It was his way of warning me not to try to pull anything because he was ahead of me. He probably pricked up his ears the moment somebody mentioned that I'd come with you.'

'If he's that shrewd,' Charlie said, 'do we want him?'

'He owes me,' Keith said. 'I know some others in the Strathclyde force, but if I got what they owed me I'd end up in the jug.'

Cathcart was waiting in a Jaguar complete with driver, but he walked with an aggressive strut to meet us as Charlie parked. 'He's going grey,' Keith said. 'Otherwise he hasn't changed.' Cathcart was a heavily built, fresh-faced man. His face had once been friendly but years of policing had set it in stern lines.

Keith moved into the back of the Ford. 'You'll have more room if I get out,' I said. I could see that the restaurant was serving afternoon teas.

'You sit in the front,' Keith said.

Cathcart squeezed his bulk in beside Keith. Charlie and I had to twist our necks to see him.

'You know who this is, of course?' Keith said.

'Of course. Good afternoon, Lord Jedburgh. And the other will be Simon Parbitter.' Cathcart opened his coat. 'I've no recording devices on me. Nor in my car.'

'I never really thought so,' Keith said. 'Inspector Cathcart never did play those games. But it pays to be careful. I'm not so well acquainted with Superintendent Cathcart, nor with his driver. Just how did you know that this was the Earl of Jedburgh?'

Cathcart's eyes narrowed slightly. It could have been a faint smile. 'I mistrust all suicides on principle,' he said. 'So I insist on minute by minute reporting. When Inspector Strachan reported the outcome of Lord Jedburgh's visit, I asked who had come with him.'

'Why?' Keith asked.

'Because I always do,' Cathcart said. 'And very informative it sometimes is. As this time. And, as you say, it pays to be careful. A suicide can be too easily faked, if the investigating officers aren't on their toes. I don't say that it happens every day and we've no statistics on the success rate, naturally; but I have my own suspicion that among unsuspected murders the fake suicide figures more often than it should. Take this case. Imagine somebody holding a gun or a knife on your man Lucas. "All I want is time to get clear," he says. "So you drink this little lot and by the time you can manage a car again I'll be well away. Otherwise I'll just have to kill you." And when Lucas is out cold, he does the job.'

'That may be exactly what happened,' Keith said, 'or it may not. There are certain indications that it may not have been suicide.'

'Then why can't you tell them to Inspector Strachan?'

'Because of the nature of Lord Jedburgh's business,' Keith said. 'You know about it?'

The Superintendent looked insulted. 'Certainly,' he said. 'It may not be my business to form judgments, but I'd have had to be blind not to have seen how many brains were being drained abroad before he set up, and how many firms have benefited from his success. And that's not idle flattery. My own brother-in-law moved up from foreman to production manager instead of being made redundant, and all because the lads at Aikhowe turned a wild idea into a going proposition, just when the designer was about to go and try the Japanese.'

Lord Jedburgh looked gratified.

'I'm glad,' Keith said. 'Because, if you see the importance of his work, you'll also see that his reputation for secrecy is his biggest asset. Who's going to come to him as a client if secrets are leaking out?'

'And are they?'

'It has happened. Once.'

'Go on,' Cathcart said. 'I'll listen. You know that I can't make any promises.'

At that point, Charlie turned white and began to make frantic signals with his eyebrows. But Keith looked away, out of the misting window at the rain which was slanting down again. From his previous dealings with Cathcart he could guess just how far the Superintendent could be pushed. He explained, in vague terms, the development of the new ammunition. 'If anybody,' he said, 'anybody at all, gets onto the market with this load before we've got our patents, it's going to be a free-for-all. We'll have lost. I won't try to persuade you that the economy outweighs a possible murder— '

'You couldn't,' Cathcart said grimly.

' —but we're hoping that at least you can help us to keep it quiet until we've had a chance to get our samples back. If we can manage that, the theft and re-covery becomes a non-event. We believe that our man's abroad by now. Whether or not Donald Lucas was his victim, we don't know yet. I'm asking you to win us a delay before any fatal accident enquiry. You can ensure that any evidence is preserved. Inspector Strachan and his boys can investigate until their hair falls out. But, just for a few days, I'm asking you to keep them away from any question of motives.'

Cathcart blew out his cheeks. 'You're asking a lot,' he said.

'I've given you a lot,' said Keith. 'And I've never let you down. Twice in the past, I've found you the answers you needed. Each time, you got convictions. Once, if you remember, you recovered—'

'I hadn't forgotten,' Cathcart broke in.

'Can you look me in the eye and tell me that you would definitely have made superintendent without those two successes?' Keith asked.

Cathcart grunted and sat in silence for almost a minute. 'That went right between the third and fourth ribs,' he said suddenly. 'Tell me what you've got.'

He listened carefully while Keith gave him an outline of the story. Keith, I noticed, was thinking furiously while he spoke. He withheld no detail of Donald Lucas's movements and passed on what we knew about Reece, but he said nothing about the bones. He described Reece's car without mentioning my fight at the roadside. When it was finished, Cathcart slipped the postcard and the hotel receipt into his pocket. 'Stay out of Lucas's house,' he said. 'I'm coming through tomorrow, to see what it has to tell me. I'll have Lucas's death upgraded to a full-scale murder enquiry.'

'You'll let us know what you find out?' Keith asked.

I thought that Cathcart was going to explode but he restrained himself. 'You want jam on both sides and no bread in the middle,' he said.

'Who doesn't?' Keith said. 'I'd particularly like to know if the blue Peugeot turns up.'

'If it does, I'll think about it. But at least I'll win you three days of grace on the subject of industrial espionage.'

'That's not very much,' Charlie said.

'It's a hell of a lot if it ever comes out,' Cathcart said.

SEVEN

After my respite from writing, in the morning I felt ready to throw myself back into it. Ideas had been bubbling in part of my mind even while I was listening to Keith and others.

But it was not to be. The here and now of reality was just fading away when I was brought back by Alice's voice at the front door. 'No,' she said, 'no and no.'

'Ask him anyway.' It was Keith.

There was not enough in the word processor to be worth saving. I switched it off and went out into the hall.

Alice, who was barring Keith's way like a mother cat defending her kittens, looked over her shoulder. 'Now look what you've done,' she told Keith reproachfully.

I kissed the back of her neck. 'Nice try,' I said, 'but you'll never be a match for this persistent pest. Keith, I have to do some work sometimes, you know. I don't have a partner to dump it on.'

It was water off a duck's back. 'Charlie wants us to go and hold his hand when Cathcart arrives,' he said.

I was about to say that they didn't need me. But the early cloud had blown away and sunlight was stroking the hills. My study was dark and uninviting. 'You're a bloody nuisance,' I said. 'But all right.'

'I've got the jeep again,' Keith said. 'Does Alice want to come?'

'Alice is busy,' she said. 'Somebody has to do some work around here.' She went into the kitchen and started banging cupboard doors.

'Charlie's a bloody nuisance,' Keith said sympathetically as he guided the jeep through Newton Lauder. 'But we'd better go and keep abreast of developments. I've just picked up a seventeenth-century blunderbuss which I wanted to overhaul.' Keith would never have achieved comparative success in several fields – as a businessman, an inventor and as a writer on historic firearms – without the neat compartmentalisation of his mind. Faced with such sudden developments in a matter intimately affecting my future prosperity, I would have been unable to think about anything else; but, having thought it over and decided that all possible activity was for the moment in other hands, he was quite capable of clearing it from his mind.

'Any more from Bill Haddo?' I asked.

'Too much. Dozens of maybes and not a single definitely after Perth. If nothing better turns up soon, we're going to have to start eliminating the hard way. I'm hoping that Cathcart has news of the blue Peugeot.'

'Time's ticking away,' I said.

'It has that habit. I'm worried, but not too worried about Cathcart's deadline. I think I can talk him into extending it.'

He would probably prove correct. It was my belief that Keith could talk a mother superior into bed with an Anglican bishop.

At Aikhowe, we had to wait under the eye of a security guard who, although past his prime, was recognisably a retired boxer and still moved with the grace and confidence of one who could look after himself.

Charlie arrived after a few minutes, dressed for work in corduroys and a stained laboratory coat. He took us into his personal office, an austere compartment in the main

93

house, carved out of a large salon by glass partitions which separated it from the cubicle of a busy secretary and another room given over to microcomputers and photocopying equipment.

'Sorry to make you wait,' Charlie said. 'I took time off to feed Donald's blasted dogs. My secretary usually does the duty, but she's busier than I am just now. I hope I'm not stuck with the beasts until Donald's estate's settled. He seems to have died intestate without any relatives closer than fourteen cousins.' He sighed and blinked at us sadly. 'We'll wait for coffee until Cathcart joins us.'

'He's still coming?' Keith asked.

'He's here, with a small team, looking over the cottage. They seem to be funking the kennels and runs, though. Can't say that I blame them. Without exercise, training or walks but with irregular feeding and no sign of their usual pack-leader, those dogs look as if they'd tear the first comer limb from limb.'

Keith stirred. 'Let's go and give Cathcart a hand,' he suggested.

Charlie shook his head. 'Cathcart's orders were quite clear. If anybody, yourself especially, goes near them, he's to be locked in a spare kennel and watched until they've finished. Until the deadline's up, he seems to have accepted that you're keeping some information back about industrial espionage; but he's damned if you're going to interfere with any new evidence.'

'I don't know why he thinks I'd do a thing like that,' Keith said. His feelings seemed to be hurt.

'He's met you before,' Charlie pointed out. 'Keith, do we have a chance in hell of saving our bacon?'

Keith shrugged. 'The only answer I can give you is a qualified maybe. Time isn't as short as you might think unless Reece already had a buyer on a string. I'd give us a fifty-fifty chance of catching up with him. Our chances of doing so before the story breaks are slender, but that's your headache rather than mine. On the other hand, Reece may get conned into parting with a small sample for testing. In which case, my wad could be copied and analysis would give the rest of the game away. We could catch up with Reece to find that he's waiting for a phone call which will never come because he's already been double-crossed.'

The Earl sighed. 'I wish I hadn't asked,' he said.

'A trouble shared is a trouble doubled,' Keith replied. 'Have you come to any conclusions about your staff?'

Charlie raised a hand in a vague, helpless gesture. 'Donald had to be a traitor,' he said. 'It all stacks up. Bones. The dog-lead. Overhearing Simon talk about his dog. He seemed eager to take over Simon's vigil.'

'And, of course, sudden death.'

'Whatever it turns out to be,' Charlie agreed. 'He could have worked the trick without any other inside help. The others all seem to be beyond suspicion. But so did Donald.'

The arrival of Superintendent Cathcart rescued them from a repetitious discussion of the Aikhowe staff, doomed to profitlessness by an almost complete lack of data.

Cathcart accepted a chair and leaned his elbows on the table. His suit, which looked new, was dusty. 'Lord Jedburgh, Mr Calder and the silent Mr Parbitter whose interest in this matter has yet to be explained,' he said, nodding to each of us in turn.

'Whenever Mr Calder's faced with anything difficult,' I said, 'he asks me to do it for him.' Keith snorted.

The Superintendent raised his eyebrows but seemed satisfied. 'It seems that the late Mr Lucas was a meticulous man,' he said. 'Too damn finicky by half. So tidy that there's hardly anything personal in the place.'

'That's exactly how he was in business,' Charlie confirmed.

'Excess tidyness may please the womenfolk,' Cathcart said, 'but I prefer a man who keeps every scrap of paper and forgets to empty his waste-baskets. I mislike a house which looks as if the occupant hadn't finished moving in. Clean clothes in a wardrobe. Books in a case, mostly best sellers and legal tomes. Food in the kitchen cupboards, much of it as bland as the place. Did he have an ulcer?'

'He did,' Charlie said. 'Did the pathologist tell you that?'

'I haven't had the post mortem report yet. I guessed an ulcer from his choice of foodstuffs. Vodka would be an unusual drink for a man with one of those.' He paused while the secretary delivered a tray of coffee. 'Tell me about Lucas,' he said.

'Let me think.' Charlie poured coffee while he thought. 'As you said, meticulous. Thorough and knowledgeable as a lawyer, never leaving any loopholes unplugged. Something about the way he trained his dogs gave me a similar impression.'

'Dogs in neat kennels outside,' Cathcart said. 'Their feed and training gear tidily put away in a shed. Unnaturally methodical for a dog-owner.'

'Training dogs is a methodical business,' Keith said. 'If you're unmethodical, you end up with a confused dog. And that could be as dangerous as hell if you're training guard dogs.'

'Oh?' Charlie shrugged. 'Unlike any other lawyer I ever met, he didn't hedge himself around with ifs and buts. He was always prepared to give a positive opinion and then to express the percentage chance of a court taking the opposite view. I liked that. What else?' Charlie asked himself. 'He was polite. But not communicative on a personal level. And always as neat as a pin, amazing in a dog-training bachelor. There was never a dog-hair on him – he had special overalls which he always put on before going near the dogs. Clean shirt, tie straight, handkerchief in breast pocket.'

'Sex life?' the Superintendent enquired.

'Until recently, he gave the impression of . . . ' Charlie stopped.

'Sexlessness? Or the other thing?'

'Neither of those,' Charlie said hastily. 'My guess was that he was inhibited where women were concerned. He looked at them a lot, flirted a little. One or two girls on the staff would have rolled over for him, but he seemed afraid to risk a rebuff. Then, a couple of months ago, I noticed a change. He said nothing, but he was happier, more relaxed and his assurance began to verge on over-confidence. And I happened to see him once, dining with a woman in Edinburgh. My guess was that she was the cause of the changes.'

'Describe,' Cathcart said.

'I'm not very good at describing women,' said Charlie. 'I'd put her at slightly older than Donald, perhaps late thirties, but she could have passed for twenty and a few at a quick glance. Black hair, slim, thin featured except for the lips. Nose a bit longer than I like in a woman, but not enough to spoil her looks. She seemed well dressed in a sexy sort of way. You know what I mean? Nothing hanging out, but a dress which seemed to show off quite a good figure almost by accident.' Charlie's hands twitched, as though they wanted to make sketching movements in the air. 'But I'm not much of a judge of women's clothes. What man is? Does any of that help?'

Cathcart nodded. 'At a guess, she's the subject of the only photograph in the place, apart from shots of his blasted dogs. I was hoping that you could offer us an identity, but apparently not. Go on about him.'

'Not much more to say. Watching him in the restaurant, out of no more than idle curiosity, he struck me as acting both suave and possessive. Neither of those would've been out of character for him, but they seemed to have taken over. He was still as controlled, but now there seemed to be something obsessive about him. Frankly, he had all the signs of a sexually repressed man who was – ah— '

97

'Getting it for the first time,' Keith suggested, 'and carried away with the sheer joy of it?'

'Something like that,' Charlie said. 'Anyway, from about that time there was a difference. Nothing you could put your finger on – don't smirk, Keith; I always said you could pick a dirty meaning out of the Sermon on the Mount – but sometimes I thought that I caught him in a secret smile. Does that make sense?'

'It makes sense,' Cathcart said. He tried to hide a small smile of his own. 'I'll tell you something. You mentioned the clean handkerchief. When we came to examine the clothes on the body, the scrap of silk showing at his breast pocket turned out not to be a handkerchief at all. It was a pair of panties, laundered and carefully folded to hide the lace and elastic.'

'How very odd!' Charlie said.

'Not so odd. Commoner than you'd think. A man carries what to him is a delicious secret and has a private laugh at every other man who doesn't know what he's seeing. Or missing.'

There was a silence while we each considered this quirk of human behaviour. Keith who, according to local legend, had very much enjoyed some promiscuous years before settling into marriage, would have had little sympathy with the wonderment of a man in his thirties who had been pitchforked into both love and sex for the first time.

'Had she been staying there?' Keith asked.

'There are no obvious signs that she'd ever been near the place,' Cathcart said. 'But we'll see what the team turns up.'

'We'd have known,' Charlie said. 'Staff are always walking around the drives here and as a rather introverted community we notice each other's comings and goings. A girl at Donald's cottage would have set the tongues wagging. I suppose it's too much to hope that you found a will? I want to get rid of his dogs.'

98

'No such luck. We'll leave the shed open for you, but the cottage will be locked and sealed until we've finished with it.' The Superintendent paused and looked at his watch. 'I must away shortly,' he said. 'I only came to get some background on Donald Lucas and to feed you one or two scraps of information, in case they're of use to you in the one day you've got left.

'Firstly, the hotel bill. He seems to have stayed at the Greenmilns Inn with a lady who, from the staff's description, must have been his inamorata,' the Superintendent rolled his tongue lovingly around the word, 'from that Friday night until some time on the Tuesday.'

'But the Greenmilns is way over towards the west coast,' Keith said. 'His postcard was postmarked Edinburgh and I thought that it said the Tuesday.'

'Easily explained,' Cathcart said. 'He gave it to the woman to post and, other things being uppermost in her mind, she forgot about it until she got home.

'Secondly, we've found the car which Reece was using.'

'Ah!' Keith said.

'Yes. The number plates had been altered, using materials you can buy from any caravan shop. The car was stolen in London about four months ago.'

'About the time Reece left his old firm,' Charlie said.

'The car turned up at Dyce Airport, north of Aberdeen,' said Cathcart. 'The front was crumpled but it was still a runner. We were lucky. The Aberdeen police had already noticed the damage to the car and when they checked the registration number they found that it didn't correspond. So when our enquiry reached them they could give us an immediate response. They've since told us that it had been cleaned out and wiped over, but we'll see what the Forensic lads make of it. One question, though. We found some of these on the floor. Do they tell you anything?'

From a twist of paper, the Superintendent decanted some tiny pellets into his palm. Keith leaned forward for a quick look and then sat back. 'Ordinary lead shot,' he said. 'Number six or seven.'

'Not some of your missing sample?' Cathcart said. 'A pity. Somebody went out of his way to get them down to me. I thought that I might be doing you a favour. The car seems to have reached Dyce around five p.m. on the Tuesday. We were lucky again; an air traffic controller noticed it because of the damage.

'There's no trace that Reece ever went out on a scheduled flight, although it will be impossible to be sure even when Aberdeen police have interviewed the remainder of the airport staff. But some of the oil companies run charter flights between Aberdeen and Texas, for staff going on leave or their families coming over, and they're not always fussy about who gets on board. Reece may have phoned a Texan friend with one of the companies, because a place was saved for a man on one of those flights and he flew out that evening and set down in Dallas on Wednesday evening, their time. The Aberdeen police managed to find the friend, but he seems to be no more than a bar-room acquaintance. According to his passport the man's name was Jenkins, but the acquaintance knew him as Roberts. The description tallies.'

Keith scowled with the effort of calculating the time difference. 'Long flight,' he said.

'The plane was delayed in Newfoundland,' said Cathcart. 'Engine trouble. If you've time to spare, go by air.' He looked at his watch again. 'And not, myself, having any time to spare . . . ' He began to rise.

'Can you win us some more time before you let the rank and file know about our problems?' Keith asked.

Cathcart got to his feet. 'As to that,' he said, 'we'll see what we shall see. And now, I must go. Yours aren't the only problems in the world.'

Charlie saw him out and came back frowning. 'That doesn't take us much further,' he said. 'But then, you didn't tell him a damn thing you didn't want him to know.'

Keith was looking blankly at the ceiling. 'I didn't tell any lies,' he said. 'Fair's fair. What he told us didn't take us a damn bit further. What he didn't say was much more illuminating.'

'I wonder whether he isn't thinking just the same about you,' said Charlie.

Keith had moved to the telephone. 'How do I get an outside line on this thing?' he asked. 'I want to speak to Bill Haddo.'

Charlie got the number for him. Keith did the speaking. 'Bill? We've got a strong pointer in the direction of Dallas. You had a possible sighting . . . ' There was a pause while the receiver muttered in his ear. 'Another one? Give me the details.'

He listened for a full minute and then looked over at me. 'This is going to take some time,' he said. 'You take the jeep and run along home. Charlie can give me a lift back later.'

The prospect of spending the next few hours listening to one side of a series of abortive phone calls I found depressing. I accepted the jeep's keys and made my escape.

I drove away from Aikhowe with the puzzles of Reece's disappearance and Lucas's death at the front of my mind, but it only took a random idea for my novel, inspired by a glimpse of a smartly dressed hitch-hiker, to return me to that world of my mind which can, for hours at a time, become more real to me than the real world. I gave Alice a summary of the morning's developments which must have been so condensed as to be indigestible and sat down at the keyboard. An hour later, when I was deeply submerged in my work and had quite forgotten Keith and his troubles, all hell broke loose.

'Keith's on the phone,' said Alice's voice.

Groping my way to the surface I first attached an identity to myself, then to Alice and finally to Keith. 'Huh?' I said, or words to that effect.

'I told him I wasn't going to disturb you for anybody less than the Queen herself,' she said defensively, 'but he wasn't going to take no for an answer. He wants to know whether you have a visa for America in your passport.'

'I have,' I said. I had been over to finish ghosting the autobiography of a pop star who was touring the States at the time. 'And if the Queen calls while I'm writing, tell her to wait,' I added. Alice is very good about defending my privacy while I'm at work, but it never does any harm to rub the message in.

'I'll let her in if she asks nicely,' Alice said and went back to the phone.

My neatly stacked ideas were blown to the winds. And, anyway, I was hungry. I recorded my work on floppy disc and called it back again, just to be sure, before switching off and wandering through to the kitchen.

Alice looked at me in surprise. 'I wasn't going to disturb you again,' she said.

'I'm hungry. Once is more than enough. It's all right,' I added hastily – Alice takes these things to heart. 'You're a pearl among women, the best sentry I ever had and I still want you to marry me. What did Keith say?'

'He's coming here.' Alice moved a snack from the freezer to the microwave and pushed the touch-pads. It beeped at her affectionately.

'It sounds as if he wants me to go to the States for him,' I said. I flopped into a chair and massaged the back of my neck. 'This is getting out of hand. I've got used to dashing all over Scotland for him, but I draw the line this side of the Atlantic. He can do his own errands.'

'I don't think he can,' Alice said. She came round behind me and took over the massage. 'He's terrified of flying. Molly told me he's convinced that aeroplanes are made of the same material as paper hankies. She got him as far as Madeira once, and it looked as if they were going to have to settle down there.' Through her fingers, I could feel Alice's laughter deep inside her. 'He came back on a cruise ship in the end. And you know you said you wanted to visit the Library of Congress. This could be your chance to get your fare paid and still claim the tax on it.' She has a natural talent for business and had taken over the administrative side of my writing, and glad I was to be rid of it. But she spoke absently. Her mind was still on my twelfth proposal. A girl may decline or even ignore an offer of marriage, but she notices it. 'You know what I said before. I'll marry you when you're more . . . one of us. I wouldn't want folk to think that I'd married some kind of an alien.'

'We're all Brits together, for God's sake,' I said. 'And, anyway, people already think we're married. Three different men have called you "Mrs Parbitter" in the last few days.'

'I wouldn't want them to know that I'm living in sin either,' Alice said placidly.

I had finished my snack and was drinking a mug of strong tea while trying to understand this latest example of feminine logic when Keith arrived at the door. I heard Charlie driving away in the Range Rover before I could get to the door and ask him in. I gave Keith tea and a seat in the living room. Alice stayed in the kitchen, but with the door casually open.

'We seem to have smoked the clay,' Keith said with satisfaction.

'What kind of metaphor is that?' I asked. 'Agricultural or drugs?' Turns of phrase are a writer's stock-in-trade.

'Clay-pigeon shooting, you ignoramus,' he said. 'Bill Haddo's a wonder. Not having much else to do, he's thrown himself into this business, broadcasting almost constantly. The problem was that you'd be amazed how many men with bruises and red hair are going around in battered, blue Peugeots and carrying gun-cases, perm any three from five. That one,' he added considerately, 'has to do with the football pools. We were waiting until the traffic died away before starting to eliminate, but what Cathcart said about Aberdeen pulled the rabbit out of the hat.'

Keith paused as if wondering whether he need explain about magicians and rabbits. 'Haddo got a call during the night from somebody who didn't want to identify himself. Probably a filial-minded customs official who had no business passing on that kind of information. Anyway, somebody bearing a striking resemblance to your description of our man, complete with swelling and a couple of teeth missing, landed in Texas on Wednesday evening. Dallas/Fort Worth, that was. Haddo says that the caller was boiling with indignation that a man should treat his mother that way.'

Regrettably, my attention was first caught by the reference to missing teeth. 'I must have swatted him a good one,' I said with satisfaction. 'Do we know where he went from there?'

'If you'd listen,' Keith said severely, 'instead of patting yourself on the back, you'd hear the rest. Before calling Haddo, he'd taken the trouble to speak to the redcaps, and one of them remembered putting the man into a cab driven by a local character, an elderly negro known as Uncle Mo. So I phoned a Texan friend. I found him a Churchill Twenty-five once. A beauty and it fitted him perfectly and when he came over to collect it I took him to shoot capercaillie. He came over again last year and I fixed him up with some stalking.'

'But you digress,' I said.

'I do, rather. Sorry,' he said, not the least abashed. 'Anyway, I phoned Earl.'

'More earls?'

104

'Earl Bell. It was early morning over there, which is a good time to catch people on the phone. He phoned a friend who phoned another friend who knew where Uncle Mo lived. Earl spoke to Uncle Mo and called back.'

'So we know which hotel he's at?' I suggested, hoping to cut a long story short and get to the subject of the many reasons why I was not going to America.

'Unfortunately no. Reece was dropped at a Dallas restaurant where, I suppose, he could get a meal, phone around for a reservation and then call another cab. Or get on the Link, which is a sort of minibus which does the circuit of the hotels.'

His concluding sentence caught my attention. 'How would you know about the Link?' I asked curiously. 'Not from the soap opera. That's all Rolls-Royces and late model Mercedes. Don't tell me you've been to Dallas?'

'No, of course not,' he said. 'Earl mentioned it. He's going to set things moving. He said that it's still hot over there. Take a light suit for evening wear, but during the day most people who aren't in offices slop around in trainers and casuals. But you'll need a wind-cheater. It's flat country and it can blow a gale.'

'Now, hold on,' I said. 'Why on earth should I go whizzing off to the States?' Keith's bland assumption that I would go blithering off to the ends of the earth at his bidding was irritating me. I sensed that something in my subconscious was determining that I was going to be awkward. It was no deliberate decision on my part but a reaction which it was beyond me to prevent.

'Well, I can't go,' Keith said reasonably.

'You mean that Molly won't let you go?' I suggested.

He jumped as if I had stabbed him. 'It's not that at all,' he said. 'I'm much too busy. And, remember, we've got a murder mystery over here and a delicately balanced relationship with Cathcart.'

'That wasn't exactly what I meant,' I said. 'Look at it this way. I don't like shooting. You've got me more or less sold about rabbit and pigeon shooting, and I accept all that you've said about pheasants even if you do make it sound as if you're doing them a favour. But if this steel shot thing cuts down on the shooting of ducks and geese I'm all for it. I don't think that they owe you anything. Why can't you leave them alone?' I sounded very pompous, even to myself.

He puffed out a big breath, which was his sign of exasperation barely contained. 'In my time,' he said, 'I've reared and released far more duck than I'll ever shoot. This isn't the time to go into all the conservation done by the shooting interests. Let me just point out that thousands upon thousands of wildfowl die each late winter through cold and starvation, yet the populations remain relatively constant because they're controlled not by shooting but by the available food supply. So, on average, a duck or goose harvested during the season represents a bird which won't die a less easy death later.'

'All the same . . . '

'Let me finish. If you're not satisfied, think about this. Steel shot isn't as good ballistically as lead. It's been proved both in theory and in practice that it results in a higher proportion of woundings instead of clean kills. Tests at Lacassine in south-western Louisiana showed a more than forty per cent increase in crippling. My new cartridge puts that right. But even that isn't really the point. The new load will come in anyway. The question is whether I reap the reward for designing it. Does that help that tender conscience of yours?'

I needed more time to digest his arguments. What cut more ice just then was that a friend was in trouble. I could have forced him to admit that he was afraid of flying but I had a sudden attack of compunction. I made a vague sound which he could have taken for assent. 'What about

Alice?' I asked. 'And Boss? We still aren't sure that Reece didn't have an ally over here.'

'They can stay with us. If you need a little extra motivation,' Keith said, 'the reason Bill Haddo's caller remembered Reece so clearly is that he's a gun buff and he took a damned good look at the Purdey. That's why I think the caller was a customs officer. Reece already had a Form Four-five-five-seven listing the dutiable things he'd taken out with him. That's the form you use so that you don't have to pay duty when you bring your own things back home again. The gun was on it. He must have added it to the list, above the signature and stamp.

'Uncle Mo confirms that Reece was carrying a light suitcase and a gunbag. If you can recover our samples, you'll be well looked after.' He stopped and seemed to be struggling with himself. 'And the reward for Sir Philip Dunne's Purdey is all yours if you can bring it back,' he finished in a rush.

'Fair enough,' I said, and suddenly it was too late to call the words back.

'That's fine,' Keith said briskly. It seemed that my hesitation had been no more than an irritating hiccup in what he had known would happen anyway. 'Your tickets are in hand. Sir Philip's putting together some papers about the Purdey, in case you have to prove that it was stolen. I'll pop you on to the shuttle rather before the crack of dawn tomorrow and you fly from Gatwick. Charlie's gone off to fix you a credit card and some dollars and a package of electronic gubbinses in case you have to listen in on somebody. If you can think of anything else you might need, let me know. And get to bed early. You've a long day tomorrow.'

He left soon after that. He had the grace to apologise for the interruption to my writing. But, he said, I would probably get a book out of it. He always says that. About once in five, it turns out to be true.

I did not feel like writing any more. I felt alone and vulnerable. No way was I going unarmed in pursuit of a crook – and, moreover, a crook whose teeth I had reduced in number – into his home territory where, I believed, a man felt undressed without a gun. I considered the walking stick gun which I had inherited from my uncle but doubted whether I could get it through Customs.

Instead, I remembered another piece of my uncle's equipment which I had put away among his other shooting gear. I took it out into the garden and found that my hand had not lost its old cunning. Feeling silly, I smuggled it upstairs and hid it in my case.

EIGHT

Next morning, at about the time when I would usually be stirring in my bed and choosing between the competing attractions of Alice and breakfast, I found myself instead riding a DC10 and wondering, not for the first time, why I allowed Keith to disrupt my life. Annoyingly the aircraft, on its 'great circle' course, headed back north over Prestwick. It could, I thought, have stopped to pick me up there and saved me the early awakening.

Alice had been deeply asleep when the alarm clock woke me. I had tried to leave without rousing her, but she had come to sufficiently to bid me an affectionate farewell. That she made only a passing request that I be careful I put down not to her sleepiness but to the fact that she knew me to be cautious to the point of cowardice.

Not even the importance which Keith and Lord Jedburgh attached to my mission had induced them to stand me a flight by Concorde, so it was a long trip and a hungry one. Travelling with the sun, the clock moved slowly and the cabin crew only seemed to serve a meal when the local time zone decreed that it was due. Although I neglect mealtimes when I am working, I am a constant nibbler during my occasional periods of leisure. When at last we dipped out of cloud and saw the cities sprawled across a flat, green landscape, I was more interested in my dinner than in any problem of Keith's.

Customs gave me no trouble. The lady on the immigration desk seemed ready to turn me back on the grounds that my passport described me as a writer and she had never read anything which I had written. Between hunger and general irritation I was in a mood to resent being looked on as a potential threat to the US Government or its economy and I snarled back at her. This probably did my case more harm than good, but in the end she wished me a pleasant trip and returned my passport with such violence that she nearly stove in my ribs.

Earl Bell was waiting for me at the luggage carousel. I recognised him from a photograph which Keith had shown me. Keith had probably described me as a thin man with brown hair and a ginger beard, but whatever his words they seemed to have conveyed an adequate picture because Earl recognised me at the same instant. Earl fitted my idea of a typical Texan, being large in every direction. He was in his early fifties with a head of silver hair. He had a round and amiable face which had become tanned without being noticeably lined. He moved and spoke slowly, but it took him only a few seconds to greet me, round me up and herd me, with my one case, into an enormous car. The afternoon was as warm as a British summer.

'First we eat,' he said. 'I'll take you for a Mexican meal like you've never known before, not a bit like the junk which passes for Mex most places, and I'll wise you up. Then you can get some sleep. I've done that trip a thousand times and I can guess how you feel.'

It was only late afternoon in Texas but I had been up since 3 a.m. and it was already mid-evening at home. My internal clock was confused but insisted that bedtime was overdue. I was content to be swept along.

Earl saw me looking at the trees and scraps of countryside – very green by our autumnal standard. 'You must come back and see it in the spring,' he said. 'By now, summer's just plain tired out. It goes on too long . . . '

110

The soap opera had prepared me for a Dallas of silver skyscrapers, but those seemed to be almost confined to the mini-Manhattan of 'Downtown' and the occasional new hotel scattered among low-rise sprawl. All the same, I envied the man who had the concession for solar glass. He could get rich without slaving over a word processor, ruining his figure and his digestion.

Earl swung off the turnpike. Beyond a residential area, he parked at a large restaurant which, as best I could see behind all the neon, was built in Spanish style. Beyond it, one of those towering hotels loomed. The place was just beginning the evening's bustle. We drank Margueritas while Earl ordered and then a mild, American beer with the meal. Remembering Montezuma's Revenge I was chary of the Mexican food, but the mixed grill with tortillas seemed to me, in my famished state, delicious beyond belief.

While we ate, Earl chatted – mainly about Keith whom he seemed to regard as no more than one rung below the Almighty, but when we had finished our meal and were toying with another beer he came suddenly to the point. 'I better tell you what we've done so far,' he said.

'We?' I had supposed that he was alone in this.

'Hell, yes. Me and three buddies that I run with. You'll meet 'em later. We live between here and Paris, about two hours away.' He smiled wryly and took a pull at his beer. 'I guess we're just a bunch of broken-down old loonies who've screwed up our health so's our companies got rid of us before we were ready for the old folks' home. Cooley did a quadruple bypass on me some time back and the others' tickers aren't up to speed.' (That, I decided, explained the unhurried movements and the absence of wasted effort.) 'So we run together, booze a little, shoot, hunt and tell lies to each other. We travel around for the shooting, but taking it easy. We don't knock ourselves out.

'Keith gave me a run-down on this guy. He sounds like a badass. Uncle Mo, the cabbie, says that he didn't ask

111

for just any place, he said to bring him here. An outsider wouldn't know about this place. When you had your run-in with him, did he talk like a Texan?'

'He talked like anybody in a Western film,' I said. 'I don't know any Texans.'

'I'm a Texan,' he reminded me gently. 'Did he talk like me?'

I fought back a yawn and forced my sluggish mind to remember. 'He sounded much the same, as far as my untutored ear could tell. I only know two accents, Bowery and the rest,' I said apologetically. 'He may have come here for advice or to get help. Or might he have come here to find a buyer?'

'He surely could,' Earl said. 'There's at least one firm out at Farmers Branch makes shot for the home-loader, and a small maker of shotgun shells in the Metroplex who'd bust a gut to be up with the big ones.'

'Where's the Metroplex?' I asked.

'This is. That's what the Chamber of Commerce calls the Dallas and Fort Worth area and all the small, incorporated cities.

'From what Keith tells me, this new load could be the answer to a maiden's prayers. Not to mention the prayers of that manufacturer, all the shooters and a dozen wheeler-dealers who'd pay big bucks to get their fingers in this pie. I'll tell you, Simon. Like it or not, this steel shot thing's going to be big. Looks like lead shot will be banned here for waterfowl by 'ninety-one. I reckon that lead shot's going to be banned altogether – not just for waterfowl but for other shooting and for skeet as well. And that's one hell of a lot of shells.

'And steel shot tears hell out of gun barrels. Browning, Remington and Winchester have all produced barrels which can take it, but they don't say for how long. Hell, they're in the business of selling shotguns and shells.' A scowl was sitting uncomfortably on Earl's mild face. 'That's fine for me and my buddies, we can afford to buy guns. The average redneck works his ass off to buy a gun and he'll have to keep it even when the barrel looks like shit from the shit he's had to put through it. Then there's the zillions of older guns still in service, are they all to be scrapped? Like my Churchill? Your Lord Whasisname's Purdey won't take steel shot long without scoring and blowing open the chokes. Did you know there's not a choke in this country can take steel shot? They can make steel hard enough, but the only tools can machine it are in France.

'Nope, my guess is that the first man coming up with a real good, non-toxic load that isn't priced out of sight will soon be up there with the Carnegies and Morgans and Du Ponts, richer than a foot up a bull's ass.'

'That's what Keith told me,' I said. 'I didn't know whether to believe it.'

His scowl deepened. 'We'd better all believe it. I'll tell you some more. There's a guy in Big Spring, Texas, started to figure out a coating for shotgun barrels. It turned out so good that he's going after the offshore and oil industry market instead, because how much stuff could he sell to coat all the gun-barrels in a shop? A half-pint?

'Me, I reckon the scare's all bullshit. Some bleeding heart bastard found shot in a duck and said, "Ah-ha, this poor little duck died from lead poisoning." Next thing, there was a report estimating that nearly three per cent of the fall flight was lost to lead poisoning. But the way those figures were taken was suspect. Californian research showed the real figure was way lower but nobody gave it any heed. Those bastards in Washington don't know doodley-shit. Their staff tells them it's an environmental issue, which is good for votes. They won't go against the tide of opinion, right or wrong. They just want to piss off the fewest voters and get re-elected.'

In his indignation, Earl seemed to be putting his quadruple bypass at risk. Like Keith, he spoke about shooting with an intensity which he would not waste on another subject. I decided to calm him down as well as return-ing to the heart of my mission. I looked around the restaurant, now filling up for the evening's trade. 'Do you suppose any of the staff would remember him?' I asked.

'That waitress remembers him,' Earl said. 'The one with the fat ass and the tits to match. I came in here at noon today and had some time to bullshit her. She remembered him for his red hair and busted lip. He was joined by some guy she'd never seen before, but sounds like a local businessman. Grey suit and ulcers. They were talking real quiet for an hour at least but she didn't see anything change hands. Uncle Mo said that Reece had him stop to make a phone call on the way here. Probably your man's first try at finding a buyer. Hell, he might talk to fifty before he hits the right one.'

'Or he might strike oil first time,' I said. 'We'd better get moving.'

'We're moving,' Earl said. 'We're moving. When they split, your man asked the girl to call him a cab. She told him that there's always empty taxis at the hotel at the back. He gave her the old bullshit, told her he'd like to take a lady like her over to the hotel for a good time; and she said she wouldn't bite his lip like the last girl he'd had. That one,' Earl said thoughtfully, 'could unscrew your left nut and never lose her breath. You know what they say . . . "A big horse rides easy."

'Anyway, he left towards the hotel. If he picked up a taxi there, we haven't found it yet, but Pete's out trying. Pete Hogan. He used to insure every fleet of cabs worth insuring in Dallas, before taxis became uninsurable. He still knows everyone worth knowing in the business, but if your man used a small operator it could take time. We've already tried the ones whose cards are up over the phones at the hotel, but no dice.

'My other two compadres, Daniel Janes and John McLaine, were both in hardware so they have some contact with the shotshell dealers and either know or are kin to all the folks in the metal industry. Also, John has a cousin works for the cartridge manufacturer. They're doing the rounds, chasing whispers. Somebody may be looking for advice or finance and somebody else may know something and be prepared to spill it.

'Only other thing we could think of was Sir Dunne's Purdey. Must be ready to shit bricks, losing it. Man could give up nooky for a fortnight to own a gun like that. For the pair, three weeks.' Earl showed signs of a rising head of steam again. 'Me, I'd kill the sonofabitch that stole it from me; not a jury in Texas would convict when they heard the story.

'There's not so many dealers in the States handle that class of gun. I've phoned Hershel Chadick in Terrell, Don Shrum in Cape Girardeau, Don Criswell of Yorba Linda and James Wayne of Victoria. Those are the boys who'd pay a proper price for a new Purdey, but none of them's seen one lately. I passed on the serial number and we'll get a call if it turns up. Most Texans seem to know the value of a gun by instinct, the way my wife can spot a diamond clear across a cocktail party and tell you the number of carats and how it's cut and how much it's worth on today's market. But if your pal Dave Reece is dumb enough to sell it to some jake-leg bastard for a fistful of bucks that don't add up to nothing, we can kiss it goodbye. There's many would buy a gun like that, hot or not, just to keep and fondle it. There's not a lot we could do about that. Not without blowing the story open.'

'You've been to a lot of trouble,' I said, 'and Keith will be grateful. Do you want me to take over now?'

'Hell, no,' Earl said, to my great relief. His ready smile was back. 'We used to be busy guys. Maybe that's what did the four of us in so early. You can only burn the candle so much, so fast. Whatever, there's a lot of days to fill and we can't shoot all the time God made. My wife's in California visiting with our son; Dan and John are divorced and Pete's a widower. We'd be pissed off if you didn't want our help. We don't get to use our minds on anything bigger than taking out the garbage any more. That and figuring out how to screw each other on a gun trade. Man, this is fun.'

'I'm glad,' I said.

He saw me fighting back another yawn. 'Yeah,' he said. 'You must've been up nearly twenty-four hours. We're booked in at the Lincoln. I'll take you there right now. I'll wake you if anything breaks.'

I slept like the dead and awoke, suddenly and refreshed, after 9 a.m. Central Standard Time. My room, which I had been too sleepy to examine the night before, was a carbon copy of every other hotel room in the States even to the picture on the wall.

I showered, dressed in slacks and a golf jacket and was on the point of leaving the room when the phone sounded. I expected to hear Earl's voice, but Keith was on the line.

'How did you find me here?' I asked.

'Earl left a message on his answering machine,' Keith said. Over the five thousand miles of telephone line, I could hear the strain in his voice. 'Don't waste time on irrelevancies. This is costing a bomb a minute. How are you getting on?'

'I've hardly got here,' I said. 'Earl seems to have done everything possible. They're trying to find the cab which Reece took from the restaurant, but no luck so far. I'm meeting Earl and his pals for a working breakfast shortly – in fact, about twenty minutes ago – and we'll plan the next steps.'

'Well all right,' Keith said. 'But it's getting very urgent. Our three days are up and Cathcart's beginning to champ

116

at the bit. I think I'll keep out of his way for a while and hope that he's gent enough not to open the bag of worms until he can find me and give me warning. Now listen. Watch your step and don't take any chances – and that message also comes to you by courtesy of both our womenfolk. For reasons which needn't ruffle your hair just yet, I'm beginning to think that Reece may be very, very dangerous. If you get close to him, make damn sure you see him before he sees you. I'd have fixed you up with a good revolver except that you couldn't have got it through Customs. Borrow one off Earl. He's got enough armament to fight a war.'

'I've got all the weaponry I need,' I said.

'If, at any time, you think Reece has rumbled you, bale out,' Keith said.

'Before or after getting your bits and pieces back for you?'

'After, if possible,' he said after a pause. 'I wish there was some way of luring him back here.'

'Tell me how,' I said.

'How the hell do I know?' he asked irritably. 'You're the novelist with all the diabolically ingenious plots and stratagems. Convince him that he's got the wrong sample, or that some big British outfit is prepared to outbid all comers. Think about it.' He rang off.

I thought about it in the lift but, frankly, I did not think much of it.

Breakfast was served in a semi-basement restaurant look-ing out over a fountain garden. Earl and his friends were already eating. They rose politely to be introduced and shook hands with great formality, enquired after my jet-lag and participated in the ordering of my breakfast.

The restaurant was almost empty by now and we could talk freely.

Nothing, either in my previous visit to the States or during my meal with Earl, had prepared me for the impact

117

of four Texans in high spirits. In years they were mature, but their enthusiasm for the chase was youthful, almost childlike and they laughed easily at the most modest joke. Earl, who was the most sober in manner, joined in the constant bantering. Once the ice was broken, I came in for my share.

Pete Hogan, the widower who had been in insurance, was a scrawny man well past middle age. To judge by his loose clothes he had lost weight and this, I decided, accounted for half the wrinkles and I put him down as being in his early rather than his late sixties. He looked at me seriously over the top of his gold-rimmed granny-glasses.

'Do you wear a kilt, boy?' he demanded.

I explained that although I lived in Scotland I had been born and spent most of my life in England.

'He talks just like a yankee I once knew,' Pete said. 'Well, I've covered the bigger companies. I don't know why we can't get taxis like you have in the UK.'

'What kind?' I asked.

'The clean kind with a driver can find his way round the first corner. Some of these companies use sand-niggers – pardon me, Arabs – instead of drivers. Unless you know the way, they'll have you lost in two blocks. Give me an old black that's been in Dallas for ever and I'll show you someone who can cut down back alleys and get 'cross town in half an hour during the rush. So far, I found two companies had cabs at that hotel around that time, give or take half an hour,' he said. 'There may be more. They had records of destinations but no one could read them and the drivers were off shift. You know the way niggers write.'

'You just uttered a bad word,' one of the others said.

'Nigger? OK, then. You know the way knee-grows write,' Pete said patiently.

'You can't polish a horse-turd,' Earl said to me. 'Pete, you don't want this foreigner to think that we're prejudiced in Texas?'

'God forbid, Pete said. 'Those drivers will come on again around noon. I'll see what addresses I can get, but your man may not be among them and I already covered most of the companies in town. I don't hold out a whole lot of hope.'

Each man, I noticed, talked loudly and leaned forward to hear. Earl saw me watching. 'Not a good ear between us,' he said. 'We were all shooters for years before ear protectors came in. The doctors call it tinnitus.'

'All it means is you can't hear worth a shit,' Pete said.

John McLaine was younger, late forties or early fifties, thickset with a square jaw made squarer by a black beard. The rest of his face had the poor colour which denotes a bad heart. He chain-smoked, spilling cigarette ash through his beard and down the front of his wind-cheater. He looked sorry for himself and was sipping a glass of milk, yet his manner was less gloomy than Pete's. 'I spoke with my cousin, the one works with Hyperload. He ain't heard shit about anyone else coming up with a new load,' he said. 'And he's working on their answer to the steel shot thing. They reckon they got an answer. But it'll cost, maybe more than the traffic will bear. So I guess somebody'd've whispered in his ear by now if they were buying in some new technology. Then I did the rounds of where the promoters and the fast buck boys hang out.'

'Your ulcer's giving you hell again,' Earl observed severely.

John shrugged. 'Couldn't hang around where the action is all evening and drink Perrier. Anyways, it was worth a gut-ache, I keep telling myself. Goddam doctor put me on a leash,' he said to me in a stage aside, 'and it's not often these guys let me off it. Beside the gut-ache, I picked up one whisper, about a dude who'd been asked to join in backing some kind of new shotshell, but no source and he's not the kind of guy you can ask. I'll go on listening to see if I can't track it further back.'

Daniel Janes, the fourth member, was as old as Pete and as tall as Earl but perhaps half the latter's weight. His head was skull-like but he had the pop-eyes suggesting a thyroid condition. He was a man of few words. 'Been around most of the hardware boys,' he said. 'Nothin' yet.'

They kicked the possibilities around while I finished my breakfast. A waitress refilled my coffee cup.

'The way I see it,' Earl said, 'is that Pete may's well go and see what he can get from the taxi drivers. John and Daniel can't do any good this time of a Saturday morning, not until the clubs and bars fill up. There isn't enough of us to watch all the doors the man might go knocking on. Besides, he could be setting up a meeting anywhere. I make a motion that we high our asses out to Dallas Gun Club, see if anybody's heard a whisper about a new load or a stolen Purdey. We might even shoot for a while – we've guns in the cars. You ever shoot skeet?' he asked me.

'Never,' I said. I decided that I might as well make my attitude clear from the start. 'My motto is live and let live. Skeet have never done me any harm.'

They roared with laughter, punching each other. Earl elbowed me in the ribs. 'Keith said you could be a funny momdicker when you wanted, but that one beats all,' he said.

All the way to the parking garage, the Texans were repeating my words and chuckling.

'Skeet never did him any harm,' John said at last. 'I guess one never flew up his kilty skirt!' And they began to laugh all over again.

For Keith's sake I would have to follow through, but I was beginning to lose faith. Given the choice of backing Dave Reece or this group of elderly schoolboys, my money would have been on Reece.

Pete Hogan went off on his own. Earl loaded the rest of us into his car, an outsize station wagon which he told

120

me could fairly be called the 'National Car of Texas'. We headed out on Interstate 35 towards Denton, took a turning which was marked only by a small sign giving the address and a warning that this was private property, and drove for another two miles to the clubhouse.

Dallas Gun Club, I learned, had sold their two previous sites to developers for healthy sums and established themselves afresh some five miles beyond the city limit, with facilities built almost regardless of cost. The clubhouse windows overlooked a row of a dozen or so clay-pigeon layouts, each with stone-built trap-houses and safety walls. These, I learned, were skeet fields. I blushed for my ignorance. Only fool's luck had saved me from disgracing myself. A blustery wind was plucking at the flying clays, making life difficult for the only group which was shooting.

Over more coffee, Earl and Daniel and John circulated, striking up conversations with the few shooters in the clubhouse. I saw handshaking and backslapping but also a succession of shaken heads. I was presented with a red baseball cap bearing the legend of the Club, which would certainly make heads turn at home. Otherwise it seemed to be a wasted visit.

'There's no Reece among the members,' Earl said as we re-entered the car. 'I did find that much out. Nobody's heard a word. Not many there, of course. Must be a big competition on somewhere else.'

'Or they didn't want to freeze their asses off,' Dan said. 'I wasn't going to shoot in that wind. It's too damn cold.'

'At home, in November, we'd call it hot,' I said.

On the way back to the road, Earl stopped the car. 'You won't have brought a gun with you,' he said. From under the dash he produced an automatic pistol, still in the maker's box. 'You'd best borrow this.'

I shrank back and kept my hands out of his way, just in case he pushed it into them. I had, once, fired a gun in anger; and I had seen Dave Reece pull the trigger of the

Purdey. Even if I had the nine lives of a cat, I seemed to be using them up. 'I don't need a gun,' I said.

'Not now you don't,' Earl agreed. 'But that guy Reece may play rough. And it'll be too late to start borrowing a gun when he's just convinced you different. You'll look funny as hell with just your dick in your hand when he gets to wanting to do a tap-dance on your head. We've each got a side-arm, just in case.'

'But how good are you with them?' I asked.

'Good enough to keep from hitting ourselves in the foot,' John said from the back. 'We do some plinking now and then on our trips.'

'Pistols aren't our weapon,' Earl said. 'Don't believe the picture shows. Most Texans don't choose pistols as a first weapon.'

'Show me,' I said.

'Why not?' said Earl.

We got out of the car. I took an empty Coke-can from the roadside and tossed it out onto the hard ground. There was nobody in sight.

I stood slightly behind them as they loaded up and took a shot apiece. I knew that I was going to show off and that I deserved to make an even greater fool of myself, but my folly over the skeet still rankled.

The spurts of grass seed marked the shots. Earl, using a heavy automatic which looked small in his big hand, was close over the top. John, with a stubby revolver, shot quickly and was away off to the right. Daniel took a two-handed grip. Despite his spindly physique his hands were the steadiest. He was low but he moved the can slightly. I had already palmed a large ball bearing. While Daniel was taking aim I drew my secret weapon and while the sound of his shot was still in my ears I let fly. I was lucky and my practice at home had prepared me. I hit the can, clattering it across the ground.

'I do that?' Daniel asked, startled.

'No way, José,' John grunted. 'You kicked a chip on to it is all.'

'I did it,' I said. I showed them my empty hands. 'Now do you believe I don't need a gun?'

'What in hell did you use?' John asked.

I took the catapult out of my pocket. Keith had explained why my uncle kept it among his shooting gear. It had been something to do with putting a decoy pigeon into a treetop, but his explanation had meant almost nothing to me.

'A slingshot!' Earl said disgustedly. 'That's kid shit.'

The silent Daniel walked to the can and brought it back. It was folded almost in half. 'Kid stuff it ain't,' he said. 'If this'd been some guy's head, which of us you think did him the most harm?'

John was nodding. 'And no noise. Nothing to show but a guy with a dent in his skull and a smooth river rock lying a long way off. I call that slicker'n snot on a doorknob.'

'I guess maybe he doesn't need a gun,' Earl said.

We returned to Dallas by a different route so that, Earl said, I could get more idea of the layout. I thought that we were almost back at the hotel when Earl suddenly touched the brakes and turned off the Stemmons Freeway, bringing the big car to a gentle halt. 'Why did nobody say this was on?' he demanded.

'Didn't know it,' said John.

'What?' I asked.

'Lookie over yonder.' Earl pointed. Beside a large building, the Trade Center, a canvas sign announced the Dallas Gun Mart. A queue of men with a few women among them, some of them carrying bagged guns, was moving steadily inside. 'Maybe that's why the Gun Club was so quiet,' Earl said. 'And if your man wants quick cash for the Purdey instead of top dollars, here's where he'll come.' He drove past and found a space in a three-storey car park.

We queued for five minutes, paid a few dollars apiece and entered a huge hall in which several hundred trade stands

123

displayed books, ammunition, militaria, loading gear and above all guns. Rifles, pistols, pump and automatic shotguns, over-unders and side-by-sides, in every quality from Best English to Saturday Night Specials.

My companions, like the addicts that they were, began to show signs of wandering off in search of their favourite dealers. John, in particular, was pointing like a gundog. I found myself pitchforked into reluctant leadership. 'Come over to the side,' I said. 'I'll take the first aisle, you take the second, third and fourth. We'll meet at the far end and come back down the fifth through eighth. Look hard at all the side-by-sides. We're looking for a brand new Purdey' – I produced Sir Philip's photographs – 'or for a macho-looking bastard with red hair and a swollen mouth.'

'And talk with the dealers you know,' Earl said. 'It mayn't be on show. Or he may come later.'

The first aisle seemed to be given over to books and equipment rather than guns, so that I was able to keep moving while watching out for Reece. If he was around, I very much wanted to see him before he saw me.

I half expected to have a long wait on my own at the far end but, apart from Daniel who had dallied to buy a copy of the *Gun Trader's Guide*, we met promptly. I set off again down the fifth aisle. I had passed only three or four more stands and was looking through a rack of what turned out to be the new Winchester side-by-sides when Earl appeared at my shoulder.

'Got it,' he said. 'It's been sold. Second aisle over, just under the Ruger sign. You want it back, you'll need cash or a cop. How do you want to play it?'

I thought it over quickly. The idea of buying back a very expensive gun out of my promised reward stuck in my gullet. And news of the stolen Purdey would hardly put a blemish on Charlie's reputation. 'Could you find a cop in a hurry?' I asked.

'No problem,' he said. 'I'll send one of the boys to find a Rent-a-cop. First let me tell you. This may not be easy. These bastards may look and act stupid, but they know quality and they can smell a stolen piece a mile downwind. The redneck sonofabitch that's holding the gun isn't fool enough to put it on show. We'd never have found him except that he had to shoot his mouth off to a dealer I've known half my life, bragging about the great deal he made in Houston.'

Earl was going too fast for me. 'Is Reece in Houston?' I asked.

'That's bullshit. That old boy's from De Soto, he'd get lost in Houston. Just listen. This peckerwood never had anything better'n a used eight-seventy to trade in his life, so my friend ragged his ass until he showed him the Purdey. My friend says it's the gun we're looking for.

'Now, boy, you go over to that table and look at the junk he's selling. If he speaks to you, just say, "I'm looking." And try not to look like a hound dog that's shitting peach seeds.'

Earl set off back towards the entrance, unhurried and yet eating up the distance. Trying very hard not to look like a hound dog shitting peach stones, I headed towards the Ruger sign.

The stand seemed to be given over to used guns which, even to my eye, looked as if they had seen a lot of mileage. I stared, unseeing, at a set of revolvers and wished that Earl would hurry. The proprietor, a red-faced man with a mean mouth, scented a customer and moved in close. His name, according to his signboard, was Billy Bob Brewer.

'Just looking,' I said. I kept my voice nasal and hoped that it would pass for somewhere west of the Atlantic.

'Them's as good a pistol as they make,' Brewer said suddenly. 'You sure do know your pistols.' (I nodded slowly and, I hoped, knowledgeably.) 'You being from out of town, I can let you have that fine little gun for only two hundred and fifty. A hell of a bargain, boy! That there's about the best there is for shooting at trash like Mexicans.' He pronounced it Meskins.

I was wondering how to extricate myself without buying any unwanted firearms when John's voice spoke from behind me. 'Two-fifty for that piece of shit? It ain't worth ten!'

Billy Bob forced a grin. 'I was just telling this here yankee' – he put a slight extra emphasis on the word – 'that I could come off a little, on account he's a visitor to our fair city.' His sharp little eyes were trying to invite his fellow Texan to side with him against the northerner.

John pointed a finger as if it had been one of the pistols. 'If he was a yankee and a visitor, you'd be breaking the law selling it to him.'

Billy Bob bridled and his eyes narrowed. 'You see me trying to take any money off him? We was just talkin' 'til you stuck your nose in. You a BATF spy?'

His last question had me baffled until I remembered that, for some reason long forgotten, firearms are lumped with alcohol and tobacco under the aegis of a single Bureau.

Earl had reappeared. 'Now, y'all just calm down. This good old boy was just showing his wares,' he said. His accent had broadened. He was playing the part of a country boy. 'Ain't that right, Billy Bob?'

Billy Bob was nodding violently but John was undeterred. I was in no doubt that he and Earl were working as a team. 'This knothead ain't got nothing but junk here. He couldn't give it away as a door prize. He wouldn't know a good gun if it bit him in the ass.'

'I know guns better'n you ever will,' Billy Bob protested.

'Granted he don't have anything worth having out for sale,' Earl said, 'stands to reason he knows guns.'

'Bullshit!' John's beard seemed to bristle in indignation. 'He ain't never had nothing and he ain't never going to have nothing.'

Billy Bob was stung on the raw. 'I might not have much,' he said, 'but I betcha I had better'n you!'

Even allowing for the fact that Texans habitually address each other in a manner which would lead to bloodshed elsewhere, I felt that the ensuing discussion would have been better conducted further away from so many lethal weapons. 'Bullshit' was the mildest expression in general use and each party had taken to referring to the other as 'Mr Shitheels.' A small audience was assembling, some pretending to study the guns, others openly listening and enjoying the run-up to a good fight.

Again Earl the peacemaker broke in. 'If my buddy here says he has better guns, you can bet your coat and ass he's telling the truth. Ain't that right, Bill?'

Billy Bob had quite forgotten my presence. 'I got lots of high-grade guns,' he said, 'but I don't lay 'em out for every shitass to finger and scratch 'em up.'

'I seen him here before,' John announced to the world in general, 'and he's never had a thing worth a dime.'

'Not my fault he got here late, after I'd sold the good stuff,' Billy Bob shrilled. 'This prick couldn't afford a quality gun anyway.'

There was a sudden silence. The insults were passing beyond the bounds of the forgivable.

'I can pay cash for any gun you got, Jack,' John said, thrusting his beard into the other's face.

Billy Bob was beginning to sweat. 'If'n I wanted, I could . . . '

'Could what?'

'Could pull out a shotgun you couldn't pay cash for, 'cause you ain't never had that kind of cash in your life and never will, Mr Poot!'

'He's bluffing,' John said and he turned away.

It was the last straw. Texan ego demanded that he back his words. 'Right,' Billy Bob shouted. 'Right, then. I'm going to show you motherfuckers one of my shotguns

127

you ain't never had enough money to buy. You ain't never even seen one of these!'

With a flourish, he took a gun-sleeve from beneath his table and extracted the Purdey. I think that every man who could see it drew breath at the same moment.

Billy Bob swelled with pride. 'An' I got two more just like this at home.'

'May I hold it?' Earl asked softly. 'Just so's I can say I had one in my hands?'

' 'Course you can,' Billy Bob said. Earl was his friend and his ally against the world. 'Don't let nobody else touch it but you.'

Earl accepted the gun and turned to me. 'This it?'

I had no need to check the serial number; every detail of the gun was imprinted in my mind. 'No question,' I said. 'That's the one.'

Suddenly, it dawned on Billy Bob that he had been suckered. 'Gimme that back!' he said. He grabbed for the gun but Earl raised it over his head and out of reach of the smaller man. 'Just a goddam minute, buddy,' Billy Bob said. 'That's my gun and I mean to have it back.'

Daniel Janes pushed through from the back of the small crowd with a uniformed guard in tow. The guard was short and elderly and fat enough for his belly to bulge over his belt. His badge and arm patch said 'Security'.

'What in hell's going on here?' he demanded.

A dozen voices tried to speak at once but when I said that the gun was stolen the word spread and silence came back.

'That gun ain't stole,' Billy Bob protested. 'I had that sombitch in stock for most of a year.'

'Show him the papers, Simon,' John said.

I got out Sir Philip's envelope and showed them the photographs, the receipt from Messrs Purdey, an insurance valuation and copies of Sir Philip's statements to the police and to his insurers. The fat guard squinted at the papers and took out a pair of half-frame glasses. He compared the serial number of the gun with that in the papers and looked hard at the photographs. 'It damn sure looks like it's the one that was stole,' he said. 'Stole just last week, in Scotland. Yurrup.'

Brewer's face was a study in consternation, but he was a quick thinker. Abandoning all previous stories he said, 'By God, I told that Iranian bastard that put the gun under my table while he went to piss, he'd better hurry back and get that ol' gun before somebody thought it was mine. Last time I try to help a man out!'

The guard began to falter. I guessed that he disbelieved Brewer's new story but was uncertain as to his own authority. 'What did he look like, this Eye-rannian?'

'You can't miss him,' Billy Bob said. 'He'd a big nose and black kinky hair and little beady eyes. He went over yonder to the pisser. You better catch the little sombitch!'

Daniel caught the guard's sleeve. 'Let's go catch him before he steals another gun.'

His enthusiasm was infectious. The two went off, followed by most of the onlookers. Earl stuffed the Purdey into the sleeve and pushed it at me. 'You got your gun,' he said. 'Now, go!'

I went. I expected Billy Bob to land on my back but, when I looked round, John and Earl were holding him by an arm apiece and Earl was speaking into his ear. Still looking back, I bumped into somebody – an elderly woman with a blue rinse and three shotguns in her arms.

'Watch your ass, you sonofabitch,' she said. 'Can't you see a lady?'

I made my way back to Earl's car which was, of course, locked. Uncomfortably aware that the cheap gun-sleeve over my shoulder housed a £20,000 shotgun, I paced around the car. My knees were shaking. The eternal Dallas wind blew through the car park, bringing grit to my eyes, while strange men with guns glanced curiously at me as they passed me by. My mood subsided from elation to apprehension. From expecting the Texans to show up at any minute I passed, as time slipped away, to envisaging all kinds of disasters. Either they had been arrested or Billy Bob Brewer had shot the lot of them.

I had just convinced myself that they had been hauled off to the jailhouse where Jack Ruby had been gunned down and that the State Troopers would be hunting me for Grand Theft Firearm, when they emerged from the stairwell. I hurried to meet them.

'What kept you?' I asked.

They were in high spirits, laden with parcels and still chortling at some joke.

'Nothing kept us,' John said. 'Except looking at a few guns.'

'Be serious for once,' I said. My nerves were overtaut. The world of guns was still a foreign land to me; despite Keith's recent influence, my London upbringing insisted that guns were for warriors and criminals.

They sobered a little. 'We're serious,' Earl said. 'Serious as a one-legged man at an ass-kicking contest.'

' . . . as your finger going through the toilet paper,' John said.

' . . . as Martin Luther King riding a bicycle through Mississippi,' Daniel chimed in, 'with a white girl on his handlebars. Hey, Simon, you ever hear about the little French girl who was ate before she was seven?'

They were all spluttering with laughter.

'For God's sake,' I said, 'will you tell me what happened?'

'I'll tell him,' John said as Earl opened the car. 'What happened was . . . I gave Billy Bob your room number.'

It was too much. As they broke up in more laughing fits, 'And fuck you too,' I said slowly and clearly. 'Fuck you all!'

130

That silenced them at last. 'I'll tell you over some lunch,' Earl said quietly. He detached the bagged gun from my grasp and stowed it gently in the car. We sat in. 'And that isn't how you say it,' Earl added. 'How you say it is, "Fuck yawl." Remember that. "Fuck yawl."'

Chortling broke out again in the back seat.

NINE

I sulked all the way back to the Lincoln. I knew that I was showing up badly, but I found it impossible to conjure up either an apology or a joke to pass it off. Daniel and John went to attend Saturday lunchtime cocktail sessions. Earl shepherded me into the hotel for lunch.

We settled at a table.

I found my tongue at last. 'I'm sorry I blew my top,' I said. 'I'm not used to all this aggro, and the needling got to me.'

Earl looked at me solemnly. 'What you said was OK, even if you didn't pronounce it right. Where you went wrong, you let them see you were riled. Never let them see that. Billy Bob got riled and look where it got him.' He gave the waitress his order and then returned to the subject. 'You know how chickens pick on one another. One draws blood and the rest attack the wounded bird until they have him run off or pecked near to death. Next time, wait ten seconds and they'll be on somebody else's ass. Often, a Texan will dish out an insult just to see if you're stupid enough to get in a fight when you're outnumbered.' It was as near to a reciprocal apology as I was likely to get.

'Is that what they were doing?' I asked humbly.

'Not quite. I'll tell you something else. We've got our educated Texans and our ignorant rednecks. There's no difference in accents, but you got regular Texas English and good ol' country boy English. Now, only an asshole or a fool or a New England yankee, which are much the same, tries to be big-time and not put everybody at ease. So we talk and act "country boy". It's our way of putting ourselves down. It's a courtesy. So don't get upset when it's your turn in the barrel. When they don't tease you, that's when you got trouble.'

'I'll remember,' I said.

He dismissed the whole subject with a quick nod. 'To get down to the nut-cutting, Simon. After you left, we gave Billy Bob a hard time. Daniel kept that guard busy. John made out he really was with the BATF, which cleared the rubbernecks away, and I played the hardass lawyer. Pretty soon, Billy would've told us his mother's guilty secret – if he'd ever had a mother.

'Trouble is, he didn't know much. At first, the things he admitted knowing you could have counted on the fingers of one foot. He admitted that he'd bought the gun from a red-headed man with a busted lip, but we knew that. Paid him two thousand for it.'

'Two thousand dollars?' I said. 'That's less than ten per cent of what it cost a few months ago.'

'So he knew it was stolen. We rubbed his nose in that and he came up with a little more. Seems he only had nine-teen hundred on him and a traveller's cheque for another hundred. Reece lent him a pen to sign the cheque. It was one of those "gimme" pens, a handout, dark blue on grey and still in the plastic wrapper. Billy Bob didn't notice the name, just the colours.

'Last thing, the redhead asked where he could phone for a cab and a man who'd just been doing a trade with the dealer next door said he was going out to Fort Worth if that would help. Reece said that direction would suit him fine and they went out together.'

'That's a pity,' I said.

Earl nodded. 'We'd've been better hunting another taxi,' he said.

133

Pete Hogan joined us before our meal was served. He was still in a gloomy mood. He was also hungry. We waited patiently while he ordered.

'This may be some help,' he said. 'I just don't know. First thing this morning I got an address and I thought, "Hey! This'll be it." But I thought I better go on in case more'n one guy took a cab from there that night. And – wouldn't you know it? – I came up with five. That's a popular place, with the shopping center at the back of it. But five! And one of those was only a street corner. Not one of the cabbies looked at his fare enough to see was it a redheaded man with a fat lip and a gun in a bag or an old lady with a harp.' Pete shook his head sadly. 'We don't even know what name he's using. So what do we do now? Watch one place each, just in case he goes there again? Don't seem possible, somehow.'

'Hold your horses,' Earl said. 'See if we can't narrow it down. Did any of those cabs go west, Fort Worth direction? Like on the Turnpike?'

'Not the Turnpike.' Pete shook his head again and sighed. 'One went to a private house near Mountain Creek Lake. Another went out past the Texas Stadium.'

'Not the airport, please God?' Earl said.

'He went out Airport Freeway but he stopped off at a motel. One of those new Windsor Motels.'

Earl gave a grunt of satisfaction. 'Didn't the Windsor chain start giving out those promotional pens not long back? Dark blue on grey?'

'I wouldn't call it grey,' Pete said. 'More a sort of dull silver. Only been giving them out a couple of weeks.'

Earl grinned happily at me. 'Then that's where we go,' he said. 'Eat up.'

I considered those words while we ate up and Earl brought Pete up to date. As we were signing for the meal I voiced my reservations. 'I can't show my face around there,'

134

I said. 'He won't have forgotten the man who knocked his teeth out.'

Pete studied me for a moment. 'You did that?' he said. 'Maybe you'll get the chance to do it again. No problem. You didn't show him your real face last time. Go up to your room and take that beard off. The weirder you look under it, the less chance he'll have of knowing you.'

'I do not look weird,' I said. 'I wear the beard because I don't always remember to shave while I'm on a writing binge.'

'Well, all right then.'

'I'll come up with you,' Earl said. 'I've got disposable razors in my bag.'

'Couldn't I keep the moustache?' I asked. 'I always fancied myself with a Mexican and they're as common as Stetsons around here.'

Earl looked at me. 'No,' he said firmly. 'Your hair's brown but your moustache comes in red like your beard. That might set him remembering. Let's go.'

When we came down again, I was depressed to know that my face, which I had not seen for ten years, now looked ten years older. My jaw was cold in the air conditioning. I felt like a first-time nudist coming out from behind his tree. But at least the mark of Reece's boot had faded. Pete took several seconds to recognise me in my Dallas Gun Club cap and dark glasses.

'Is that what you call not looking weird?' he asked sadly.

I said that it was.

'You're living in a dream world. Well, at least you can pass for one of us, until you open your mouth. Best let us do the talking or you'll have them all asking what part of England you come from and did you ever meet their Uncle Joe.'

We left notes at Reception for John and Daniel.

★   ★   ★

The Windsor Motel was of modest size, a not unsuccessful attempt to present a homelike image to attract the many who disliked the impersonality and the prices of the big hotels. It had about 40 rooms on two floors around three sides of an area of car parking and scraps of garden.

Earl parked his car where John and Daniel would be sure to see it, outside a coffee shop on the other side of the dual carriageway. We took seats in a booth from which we could watch the front of the motel. We drank coffee until I was almost ready to switch to the herbal brews which the Americans believe to be tea.

'Your pal may not be staying there,' Earl said. 'He could've been visiting with his buyer. Maybe we should check out the guests and see if we can spot anybody connected with ammunition. Or maybe Pete should go around the cab companies again, offer a reward to any driver who puts us back on Reece's tail. Seems he's still depending on taxis.'

'I done enough of that,' Pete said. 'I've been round more crummy offices than you'd believe. Your turn. I'll tell you who to speak to. Mention my name if you want to get dumped on. If the guy was wanting to be hard to follow, he could've walked from here. There's a Holiday Inn just up the road.'

'Americans don't walk,' I said. 'They're famous for it. You don't even have sidewalks around here.' It seemed to me that we were talking just to keep our mouths occupied while wondering what to say.

'They don't walk far,' Earl admitted. 'So he'll not be so far off that we won't see him go by. Unless he was visiting. Or unless he was making sure he threw off the likes of us. He could have walked to the Holiday Inn to pick up another cab.'

My spirits fell even further. Although luck had been with us, it could never last. Sod's Law dictated that Reece had only been here on a visit. When I leave the worlds of

fiction and history and am dragged out to face the real
world, I have no faith in my ability to cope with it. So I
drift with the tide. The tide, assisted by Earl and his cro-
nies, had been favourable. But tides turn – about every six
hours, I seemed to remember. We were up against a dead
end – clichés began to parade through my head – clutching
at straws, chasing wild geese up blind alleys. Rather than
stare at the unchanging front of the motel, my impulse was
to give up and go home. Keith, I thought, had a bloody
nerve. I watched without interest as a couple came out of
one of the units, climbed into a Volkswagen and puttered
off towards the Freeway.

Daniel and John arrived together after another half
hour. I felt a pang as John's face came through the door
and he saw my beardless state, touching his own beard for
reassurance.

They turned my mood round again. 'He's dealing with
Hyperload for sure,' John announced after he had got
over the first shock of my new appearance. 'Well, almost
sure.'

'Along with a dozen others?' I asked.

'I think not. My cousin was going to work the weekend
on the new load, but he was suddenly told to lay off. There
was a meeting this a.m. behind locked doors. And there's
been some discussion with the tyre depot next door about
taking over their space.'

'We're too late,' I groaned. 'He's sold it.'

'Not yet,' John said. 'I've seen how these things go
down. It takes time. The seller's afraid of being ripped
off, the buyer's half expecting a con. They're neither in a
position to go to law afterwards. So they take it by stages.
Stage One, a first contact. That was the meal when he got
off the plane. If it looks like they may have a deal, they
move to Stage Two. He hands over material which can be
checked, laboratory reports and such, but not enough to
give away the whole process. Stage Three, if it still looks

good, he hands over the rest of it and walks away with his pieces of silver.'

'When the hell did you ever see that sort of a deal go down?' Earl asked him.

John winked but said nothing.

'Stage Three could have been this morning,' I said.

John shook his head firmly. 'Nope. A deal like that, with big bucks, takes time. Unless the buyer's a one man business, there's too many have to agree it. It's a board decision. Anyway, if he was selling out this morning he couldn't have been hocking your noble pal's pet scattergun. Wouldn't've needed the bucks in any hurry, either.'

That seemed reasonable. 'If we'd been quicker off the mark,' I said, 'we might have got into Hyperload and bugged their boardroom.'

'You know anything about bugs?' Daniel asked.

'Not a thing,' I said. 'But I was given a package of electronics and a miniature camera before I flew out. I don't think they put in a suicide pill, but there's everything else. I'm told that there's full instructions inside.'

'And you haven't even opened it?' Daniel said incredulously. 'Hell, I'd've had it out and bugged everybody I knew, just for the hell of it. You got it in the car?'

'It's back at the hotel,' I said.

'I'll go get it. We've nothing else to do while we wait for the guy to show. May as well look it over.'

'Daniel always did see himself as a private eye,' Earl said slowly, 'and he always loved a gadget.'

'I was in electronics before I went into hardware,' Daniel said. He looked at me with his pop-eyes. 'You coming?'

'We'll be moving soon enough,' Earl said. 'Could that be the guy over there?'

I had taken my eyes off the motel. When I looked, Reece was getting out of a grey car, large by our standards but medium sized as American cars go. Our fight had been four days earlier, but the swelling around his mouth was still clearly visible. All the same, he looked pleased with himself. He unlocked a unit in the middle of the lower floor and went inside, shutting the door behind him.

'Got himself a rental car,' Earl said. 'See the sticker on the rear licence plate? You stay here, I'm going across.'

Earl had a half-mile drive instead of what would have been a fifty-yard walk, if a pedestrian could have crossed the busy road. But he was back after ten very long minutes. 'Reece is booked in for a week,' he said, 'under that name. I've taken three units. Put down some cash and used a dummy name.' He laid keys on the table and pushed one towards me. 'We're used to bunking in together so Simon can have one to himself. Now let's think ahead. What's the chances of a master key to fit the place?'

John picked up another key and looked at the maker's name. 'Janus,' he said. 'Harry Dingle's still the agent, right?'

'Right,' said Daniel.

'But will he play ball?' Earl asked.

John looked at Daniel. 'Has Harry's wife found out yet that he's humping her sister?'

Daniel shrugged. 'He's still walking around in one piece.'

'Then he'll play ball. Even during the weekend he'll play ball. That's one tough lady, Harry's wife. I'll get on it now.' John stood up and looked down at me. 'The things I do for this shitass! If I get the master key, Simon, you lend me the Purdey for a day or two. I could shoot a great round of skeet with that gun.'

'Bullshit!' I said. 'You'd have to club them with the butt.' I was beginning to learn the language. John grinned at me and walked out.

Earl gave me a tiny nod. 'You stay and watch,' he told me. 'Rest of us'll go back to the Lincoln, pack up and check out. Should be back in an hour.'

'I'd rather you stayed and watched,' I said. 'If you don't mind. You could follow him up if he moves. And there's no way I'm drinking any more coffee.'

I rode to the Lincoln with Daniel who, once he had satisfied himself that I could tell him no more about the bugging equipment, lapsed into the silence which he usually accorded me. I guessed that he found me as strange and outlandish as I found him and his friends. We packed for Earl and John, I settled our bills with Charlie's credit card and I rode back with Pete. Even his gloomy utterances were preferable to Daniel's silence.

The motel was less than half full. Given a free choice of units, Earl had chosen three together on what he called the second floor and I persisted in calling the first. Our units were on a balcony reached by way of a staircase in an internal angle of the courtyard, so that we could come and go without being observed from Dave Reece's window for more than a second or two at a time. We took occupation at intervals while Reece lurked in his unit below and the grey car sat idly on the tarmac.

We convened for more discussion in my unit – this time, thankfully, without the need to consume any more coffee. While we talked, Daniel eviscerated the parcel of electronics. This was about the size of a shoe-box but contained what seemed to be a full spectrum of surveillance gadgetry. I took out and examined the only item which was within my comprehension, the miniature camera.

'No good busting in on him,' Earl said. 'He may have your pal's doodads with him, but if he's got a dimesworth of sense he's stashed them with a pal or mailed them to himself. So we'd blow the whole thing. We'll have to look through his room.' He cocked an eye at me. 'You want to drive one of our cars? Or do we rent one for you?'

'Either way, I'm not keen,' I confessed. 'Not in your traffic. I've driven on the right often enough in France, but a right-hand gear change throws me when I'm trying to think everything else back to front and looking for signs and traffic lights where they don't belong. And in an automatic, I keep hitting the brake in mistake for a clutch and standing the car on its nose.'

'Then I guess you're elected to go through Reece's unit,' Earl said.

'Hey, this is some real good stuff!' Daniel said suddenly. He produced an ear-shattering bleep and killed it again. 'This here's a monitor for a magnetic homing bleep. I'll stick the homer under his wing, soon's it gets to be dark.

'They've only given us two of the monitors, and we're five guys and four cars, so here's what I suggest.' In his enthusiasm, Daniel was becoming quite garrulous. 'There's no point watching Hyperload, we wouldn't know who to follow. So we wait until Reece goes out. One of us – you, Earl? – takes one of the monitors and follows him. He also takes this.' Daniel took the miniature camera out of my hands. 'From the notes, this is an eavesdropping gismo. You run the wire up your sleeve, stick the plug in your ear, point it at your target and switch on. Simple, huh?

'Simon goes in, if John's come up with a master key. Simon, you better have this. It's the real thing.' He handed me another camera, apparently identical to the first. 'Of the rest of us, one – me? – parks near the motel entrance, the other two park where they can, somewhere near each end of the block. One of them has the second receiver, the other has to keep his eyes peeled. If the grey car comes back before Simon's out, they flash me and I swing once around and park, making plenty noise, to let him know to get the hell out.

'If there's nothing in the unit, we go through his car tonight. Not that he'd leave anything important there, but at least we could plant an audio bug. Then we can listen if he does a deal in his car.'

'The stuff's probably in his pocket,' Earl said.

'I doubt it,' I said. 'It's not a big package but there's some weight in it. No man likes that in his pocket, pulling his clothes out of shape.'

141

Daniel was still playing with the toys. 'While you're in there,' he said to me, 'you replace the microphone in his phone with this.' He showed me a small disc. 'It's what they call an infinity bug. Once that's done, we can listen in on anything said in the room, whether his phone's in use or not.'

He was moving too fast for me. 'Hold on,' I said. 'He's supposed to be an electronics whizz. If he sweeps the room and finds it, we've warned him off.'

'Doubt it,' Daniel said. He lowered himself carefully on to his knees and began to wire what seemed to be a small cassette player into the phone while speaking over his shoulder. 'He'll have done that already and he won't bother again unless we set him worrying. And if he only gets around to doing it now, I read somewhere that around one in three hotel rooms already has one of these in the phone, left over from some previous surveillance. They're cheap, so when the job's over the private dick decides it's safer to leave it in place than to go back for it.'

'Sounds like the best bet,' Earl said.

I practised fitting the bug into my phone. I am not good with my fingers and my clumsy efforts sent Daniel up the wall. 'You drive my car,' he said at last. 'I'll go in.'

'You wouldn't hear a jet-plane outside, let alone a car,' Earl said. 'And what if Reece finds Simon farting round the car park like a drunken idiot? Let him keep trying.'

I kept trying. I was becoming almost proficient at a task which any small boy could have done in his sleep when John arrived. He brought a master key and a hilarious but unrepeatable story about Harry's reaction to the blackmail. This effectively ended our conference by triggering another round of anecdotes.

The wind had dropped and there was warmth without heat in the late afternoon sun. To the disgust of the Texans, I took a chair out onto the balcony and set it where, despite the passing traffic, I could still catch the conversation as well as the sun. Many of the stories could find a place in my novels at some later date.

'Hell, no Texan goes looking for the sun,' Earl said. 'He looks for shade. Only northerners go out in the sun.'

'Then I'll just have to pass for a yankee,' I said. The chance of a little sunshine in November was too good to miss.

'You don't want to be taken for one of them,' Earl said.

Reece's car pulled out at seven thirty and we went into action. Our four cars scattered and I saw Daniel reverse into position near the motel office. It was dark and the floodlighting of the car park left lakes of shadow which came and went, chased around by the lights of the passing traffic. Heart in mouth, I took the master key and let myself into Reece's unit.

The sight, the feel, the very smell of the place took me back to a Scottish roadside where I had looked down the barrels of a very expensive gun . . . and where I had lost my nerve and babbled, giving Reece the very hints which he most needed. The imprint of a powerful personality was there. I could not have put my finger on any specifics, yet something in the room's atmosphere made me feel inadequate, emasculated and stupid. I pushed emotion aside and hoped that reason and logic would be enough.

I started with the phone. The infinity bug dropped into place without difficulty. I slipped the original microphone into my pocket and looked around.

Beside the phone, a small telephone notebook had been left open at the Cs. This, I assumed, was deliberate because the book was held open at that page by the corner of a small cassette player. The writing was square, forceful and uncompromising. There were only three numbers on the page, with no names or addresses against them. I copied the numbers onto an envelope from my pocket and then used the miniature camera to photograph every page.

The room itself was very tidy. There was no clutter, no scatter of odds and ends, no photographs or letters. Indeed, as I searched I realised that there were no personal oddments at all. As a man on the move and often outside the law, Reece confined his possessions as far as possible to the essentials for living. There was a neat box containing tools and some electronic components which looked similar to the ones from my case. I took some more photographs. Beyond that, nothing. One razor, one toothbrush. Changes of clothes all clean and very little worn. Apart from his dimensions and his taste in clothing, nobody but a forensic scientist could have learned anything about the man. The waste-basket was empty. I was reminded of Cathcart's description of Donald Lucas's cottage and wondered whether some common quirk of character had drawn them together.

Keeping my ears open for the sound of Daniel's car, I began to delve deeper; but by the time I had removed – and carefully replaced – the lid from the w.c. cistern, the panel from the bath, the back from the vanitory unit, the front from the air conditioner, the floor from the wardrobe, the shades from the light fittings and the drawers from the chest I was as sure as anybody could be that Keith's treasures were not in the place.

I went round once more. Shot could be poured into some hollow object. I shook the little cassette player, his aerosol of shaving cream and any other container however unlikely, but nothing rattled or felt unduly heavy.

For the last time, I examined the room. I had been there for a full hour, yet I was sure that unless Reece had been up to tricks – and I had been unable to spot any hairs or fibres in unlikely places – my intrusion would remain undetected. The cigarette ends in the ashtray and the lingering smell of smoke suggested that Reece would not be sensitive to any change in the air. I switched the lights off, on and off again and as I left I saw Daniel's headlamps flash once. All clear.

Back in my unit I followed Daniel's instructions, picked up the phone, dialled the internal code and the number of Reece's unit and allowed his phone to ring half a dozen times in the deserted room. According to Daniel, that was all that was necessary.

John and Daniel and Pete came in one at a time, and each time I had to repeat the one word. 'Nothing.'

'But the bug's in place?' Daniel asked.

I said that it was.

He listened to the silent monitor and frowned. He had the restlessness of a man whose new television arrives while all the channels are dead. 'Go down and knock on his door,' he suggested. 'That should come over, loud and clear.' But even as he spoke, the monitor in Pete's pocket began to buzz. Daniel took it from him and switched it off. 'He's on the way back.'

The grey car swept into the courtyard and pulled up with a yelp of tyres. A car door slammed. Clearly over the monitor on the telephone we heard Reece enter his room in a rush and slam the door. Daniel raised a wrinkled thumb. At every sound in Reece's room a little light flickered and the two reels of a cassette turned. We heard him moving around, performing activities which we could not identify.

'Big deal,' Pete said.

Earl's car cruised gently into its slot and a minute later the big man came in. 'Nothing,' I said yet again.

'Nothing?'

'Nothing,' I repeated. I was getting tired of the word. 'Rien. Nefas. Niente.'

'Hereabouts we say "Nada", the Spanish. He went to dinner,' Earl said. 'Alone. Straight there and straight back. Only the waiter spoke to him. Then he looked at his watch and left in a hurry.'

'Doesn't sound like much to hurry for,' Pete said. The loudspeaker was emitting small clicks and grunts.

'Expecting a phone call,' said Earl. 'Well, at least I got fed. Now you-all can go and feed your faces in turns.'

'Hold on!' Daniel said. 'He's picked up the phone.'

We heard the motel operator come on the line. 'I want an overseas call,' Reece said. The well-remembered voice could still send a shiver up my back. 'The number's oh double one double four— '

'That's the UK,' Earl whispered.

'He could have another client there, please God!' I said.

We had missed the rest of the digits. We heard the signals as the operator touched the keys. There was a delay before a ringing tone sounded at the far end. Then it stopped and a woman's voice, or a boy's, said, 'Good morning.'

If it said any more, it was drowned by a shrill crackle on the line. The connection must have been broken, because I heard Reece grunt and replace his receiver.

'What the hell was all that?' Earl asked.

'I can guess,' I said. 'Wait and we'll see if I'm right.'

Reece called the operator again. 'Ma'am,' he said, 'that was not the right number. I'll check back and make another call tomorrow. Would you call the overseas operator and get me a credit for the call?'

'I'll do that right away,' the operator said.

'There we are,' I said. 'He'd made a date to phone somebody at nine p.m.. He didn't know that he'd have money from the gun, so he was doing it the cheap way. She – I suppose it was a woman? – answered and said "Good morning," which was a signal that all was well and no message to pass. So he hung up. A complete exchange of status reports in about one second. Then he claims the number was wrong and asks for a credit. The overseas operator checks the computer and sees that the call was short enough to confirm his story. So she wipes the information off the computer and there's no charge to go on his bill.'

'There's no record of the call whatever,' Pete said. 'That's some trick! What about that noise?'

'You get noises on the line sometimes,' I pointed out.

'Not like that,' said Daniel. He wound the tape back and played it again. I jotted down the rest of the number on my envelope. 'High-speed Morse, you think? Maybe with a voice on top of it?'

'You got a slower speed on that thing?' Earl asked.

We studied the instructions. The cassette recorder had three speeds and we had been using the fastest. We wound the tape back again and played it slowly. A confusion of booming noises was Reece's movement around the room. We heard the phone lifted and then Reece spoke to the operator in a rumbling groan. The ringing tone was deep and hollow like a distant gong. Then the woman's voice, low and rasping, followed by the noise.

'That's not Morse,' Daniel said. 'That's pure, electronic noise. Either a fault on the line or he sent something coded. The person at the other end plays it into a computer.'

The digits which I had noted down looked familiar. On the other side of the envelope were the numbers which I had copied out of Reece's book and Reece had just dialled one of them. 'The careful sod didn't put down any names,' I added. 'Just the numbers. But this was on a page of Cs. I'll pass it on to Keith when I phone him.'

'Let me see.' Ed took the envelope out of my hand. He consulted the telephone directory. 'Thought so. The third number belongs to James J. Cullingpepper. He's the boss at Hyperload but he's into a dozen other deals, some of them mighty near the knuckle. He's a Bostonian, could pass for English if you didn't know better.'

TEN

I telephoned to Keith's house in the morning. It was already almost lunchtime in Scotland but, the day being Sunday, Keith was at home. While Molly was fetching him down from his workroom I had a few words with Alice, words which only increased my homesickness. The weather, she said, was cold and wet. I was already tired of the unnatural warmth and wanted no more than to get back to the pleasant rigours of a British winter with all the joys of being indoors while the weather was doing its worst outside; open fires, a hot bath after a walk on the rainswept hill and perhaps a roll on the hearthrug with Alice. I tried to tell her some of this in the few precious seconds available to us.

Keith came on the line. He took the news of the recovery of Sir Philip Dunne's Purdey quietly. I guessed for the first time that Keith would never have offered me the reward if he had thought that I had a hope in hell of claiming it. I heard the strain in his voice give way to relief when I told him that we were in close touch with Reece, had searched his unit and bugged his room.

'I wish I could give you a lead as to what to do next,' he said. 'But you're the man on the spot. I have to depend on you. How long's it going to take?'

'That's out of our hands,' I said. 'It depends how long it takes him to set up a deal. When he gets your samples back from wherever he's got them stowed away, we should know it. Then we pounce. Is Cathcart chivvying you?'

'Not a word, and I wish I knew why. Most likely, he'll suddenly arrive and say, "Time's up." If that happens, I might buy one more extension if I can promise a result in short time.'

'Promise it anyway,' I suggested. 'If I can't deliver, you're no worse off. If you want to put Reece into Cathcart's hands, now might be the time to get one of your pals in the British ammunition industry to phone him and say that the firm's prepared to outbid all comers.'

'Nice thought. But no. Not unless you can cook up a story to explain how we knew where he was. A phone call might start him wondering who else knew his movements. I think we'll just have to put our trust in you and God, in that order.'

I played him the tape of Reece's phone call. He recorded it and confirmed that he had it safely on cassette. I suggested that he ask Cathcart to trace the number. Keith said that he was avoiding having words with the Superintendent but that he might approach him through Charlie.

When we had finished, Molly came on the line. 'Are they looking after you all right out there?' she asked.

I was surprised at her concern. 'Lap of luxury,' I said. 'I'm getting coffee-logged and their tea tastes like garden refuse, but otherwise I'm fine.'

'Well look after yourself. I don't know how that husband of mine always manages to persuade people to dash around doing his bidding, but he does. Alice is worried, but she won't let on. She doesn't want to let you down. Are you sure you're not going to get yourself into any danger? I'd like to reassure her if I can.'

I explained that I was accompanied by four Texans, all armed to the teeth. I omitted to mention that the Texans were past the first flush of youth, far from fit and, to my jaundiced eye, not wholly sane. I only said that they seemed to get results, which was true.

149

When the call was finished, I settled down to the boredom of listening to Reece switching from channel to channel in the faint hope of finding some television worth watching on a Sunday morning not far from the Bible Belt.

For those of us in Dallas, the waiting extended to two more nights and a day, during which Dave Reece hardly left his room. We ate and slept in shifts, took turns listening to the sound of his movements or following him when he went to eat in nearby restaurants. Pete went out to get my photographs printed and we puzzled over the telephone numbers without being able to determine more than the exchanges in America or in the UK. Between times, we bickered over which channel to watch on the Pay TV. I spent a lot of time on the balcony, to avoid the cigarette smoke.

Earl whiled away an idle hour by getting out Sir Philip's Purdey for a loving clean and oil with the other Texans advising, supervising and commenting. When Earl repeated his earlier remark about giving up sex for a stated period in exchange for owning a similar gun, Daniel humphed loudly. Daniel, I had heard, owned more than a dozen shotguns, all over-unders and virtually identical.

'I'd trade that hunk of metal for one good hard-on,' he said.

'Only one?' Earl said. 'That's a poor trade.'

'At my age,' said Daniel sadly, 'that's all I'm likely to get. Scatterguns I can raise any time.'

Late on Sunday evening, Reece received a phone call which had us guessing.

'Honey?' said a woman's voice. 'I just got your message. It's all happening the way you said?'

'That's right,' Reece said. 'Just that way. You still going to Florida?'

150

'Got to. I'd like to be here when you may need me, but you know how it is.'

'I know.' In his voice was none of the old arrogance. Reece sounded almost sympathetic.

'Will it be over when I get back?'

'That I can't say. Depends how soon the other side moves. I guess that depends on how quick they can put together the cash. When you get back, if it's over and it's gone bad, if I've been crossed up, there's one person could have set me up and that person knows too much to go on walking around. You'll know what to do about that?'

'It'll be a pleasure,' she said. 'The thing I've got here?'

'That very thing.' The line was silent long enough for the tape to stop. 'Listen,' Reece said suddenly, with what seemed to be real warmth, 'you know you're the one for real? Don't you?'

The woman sighed. 'With you, who can tell? All I can do is trust you. Maybe I'm stupid, but that's the way it is. I'll be back later in the week. See you then.'

'Yeah.'

On the Monday, in the late afternoon, we had a brief excitement. Pete, whose turn it was to watch the great outdoors from the window of a darkened unit, rang through to say that a man was sitting in a silver Cadillac outside the coffee shop. We each took a look.

'He may be waiting for his wife,' Earl said.

'Pete says he's been there for an hour,' Daniel said. 'Nobody waits that long. Not for a wife. Whose turn to follow if Reece goes out?'

'Mine,' said Earl. 'I'll watch it. If that guy follows him I'll stay well back.'

After another half hour, Reece went out. The Cadillac seemed to be in no hurry to move so, after a discreet interval, Earl followed Reece. The Cadillac drove off, returning a minute later along the nearer carriageway to pull up in front of Reece's unit. A large man in a pale raincoat got out. We heard clicking and scratching as he picked the lock. Then he was moving around inside. Remembering my own visit, I could follow almost every move he was making. At last, with a grunt of annoyance, he let himself out and the Cadillac drove away.

Reece took his time. Earl arrived back about ten minutes after him. 'I found him again by using the bleeper,' Earl said. 'That's a great gadget. I'll have to put one on Jeanne's car. He had catfish along at the Finer Diner. What went down here?'

'He searched the place,' I said. 'He didn't seem to find anything. And he left our bug alone.'

'Reece's buyer,' John decided. 'Trying to get himself a better deal.'

Despite the sign that the deal was progressing, Pete, in particular, was losing morale. Pheasants were calling to him, or the whitetail deer in New Mexico, while he was stuck in a motel unit, waiting for something which would never come. The others suggested patience, but I could see that Daniel also was beginning to fidget.

Then, on the Tuesday morning, Reece's phone rang. The monitor still being in my room, I phoned the others and we were gathered by the time the short conversation ended. I played back the tape.

'Yes?' said Reece.

The voice which spoke came close to the mid-Atlantic accent cultivated by international actors. I could detect a trace of American, but to an American it could certainly have sounded English. I was in no doubt that this was Mr Cullingpepper, formerly of Boston. 'No names,' he said. 'You know who this is?'

'I know,' said Reece. His voice was suddenly tense.

'Right. Your lab reports check out and a friend in the Department of the Interior can fix approval. We've raised finance and can meet your figure. So we'll play this much the way we said. You want to be protected. I want to be

152

protected. And my backers are going to make damn sure they're protected. You know what I mean?'

'I can guess,' said Reece.

'So can I,' John murmured. 'Organised crime laundering hot money.'

'Ssh,' we said.

Cullingpepper's voice was speaking again. 'So if there's anything sour about this deal, now would be a good time to back out.' He waited but Reece said nothing. 'Right. Understand one thing. You hand over the samples and the rest of the process and then you stick around until we've proved that we've got the goods. Try to move on before we tell you and you may find yourself moving somewhere you won't much like, in a generally downward direction. After we tell you, you can go where you like and start spending.

'Here's how we play it. A joint account has already been opened in our two names at the Wynnewood branch of the Merchant's Bank. You go in there and give them a specimen signature and that's it. Withdrawals can only be made on both signatures.

'My agent will meet you. You'll both be alone. You'll be handed a certified, cashier's cheque which can only be paid into that account. That means that even if we took it back off you two minutes later we'd still need your signature to recover the money. Got it?'

'I got it.'

'Are you sure you still wouldn't rather have cash?'

'Nice try!' Reece said. 'But in my shoes, would you? Your hoods could take it back off me ten seconds later. And I wouldn't want large notes. Do you have any idea what a sum like that weighs?'

There was a moment of silence on the line. 'We'll do it your way,' the other said at last. 'You'll also be given a letter confirming our deal. Carry an envelope addressed to yourself and you can mail it right away. We're playing it straight but that way, if there was any malarky, you're protected. How do you like it?'

'I like it,' Reece said. 'Provided that we meet in public.'

'Thinks he'd get snatched,' John whispered.

'Damn right,' said Earl.

'You give us it all,' Cullingpepper's voice said. 'Try to keep something back and you're in deep trouble. Be at the place we agreed at eleven thirty. Make damn sure you're not followed. Top level, central atrium, the hotel side.' The connection was broken suddenly.

I looked at Earl. 'The cautious, canny, conniving bastards!' I said furiously. 'They didn't say the place. Could we follow him, using the bug, without being spotted?'

'That's for sure,' Earl said. 'But if we don't have him in sight, it takes time to find the car again. And if by then he's on foot . . . '

'He's calling out,' Daniel said.

We heard the ringing tone at the far end. It seemed to go on and on. Finally it was answered by a woman's voice.

'It's me,' Reece said. 'We're in business. You got the package safe?'

'Couldn't be safer,' said the woman. 'You're collecting today?'

'Eleven thirty. Where we agreed.'

'The Western— ?'

'No names!' Reece said urgently. 'Just bring me the package, around eleven twenty, in the hotel. You wait below, like we said. If there's any tricks I'll get it to you and you get to hell out of there and don't hand it over to anybody but me. You understand?'

'No problem. And then we can go away?' I was beginning to recognise the Texas accent from all others and this was it.

'I'll have to stick around a day or two,' Reece said. 'After that, where do you fancy? Honolulu?'

'Whee!' she said. 'That'd be the most. Honolulu and you!'

'It's going to happen,' he said. 'This time, it's going to happen.'

The call ended and we could hear Reece moving around, packing his case.

'We'd better move,' I said. 'We daren't lose touch now.'

Earl was looking smug. 'No hurry,' he said. 'You heard them. Top level. Central atrium. Only one place that could be.'

'Western something,' I said. 'Have you figured out Western what?'

'Not Western,' Daniel said. 'Westin. The Westin Galleria. Sounds right to me. I was telling myself the Galleria before she even said the other bit.'

We packed our bags, paid the bill and loaded our luggage into the cars. It seemed unlikely that Dave Reece would relinquish his retirement ticket without a struggle, and if there were any kind of fracas at the Galleria it might be politic to make ourselves scarce in a hurry while, if we failed, the Windsor Motel would be out of bounds.

By eleven, we were at the Galleria – a luxurious shopping complex on four floors, not far from the Lincoln Hotel. Internally, the Galleria was irregular but roughly linear in plan. The open wells were surrounded by a gallery at each level, backed by shops which ranged from the humble drugstore to an amazing emporium which dealt in historic documents and those in the handwriting of the famous or infamous. There, I was tempted to turn aside and browse until Earl reminded me of my bout of temperament when he and his buddies had been distracted by guns. I glanced over the railings and found that I was looking down onto an ice rink where skaters were taking lessons while others circled around the small class. All about was gloss and sparkle. The overall impression was of airiness and of the quality which denotes spending power.

155

We gathered near the central atrium at the topmost level. There were few shoppers around although trade was beginning to build up. The Texans were unusually subdued, but I recognised it as the calm before the big game.

I was far from happy. 'If the financiers are who John thinks they are,' I said, 'they're not going to let Reece out of their sight with a cashier's cheque until they've got their hands on the stuff. Signatures can be faked. It's still not too late to call in the cops.'

'Horseshit!' Earl said. 'When Keith spoke to me, before you came over, he said you might start to think like that. He said it was OK to use the cops if that stolen gun showed up, but not on the other thing, not this side of desperation. Once you call the law, you've made sure of just the sort of shit his pal wants to avoid.' Earl paused and looked at me reproachfully. 'Seems to me that Keith's more concerned over his pal's reputation than over his own money.'

'If we get the stuff back, it won't matter. A secret lost is bad news, but a secret recovered is almost good publicity.'

'And if we don't connect? If Reece spots anyone watching, he may duck out and try for another meet. Nope. The worst that can happen is they send a couple of hoods along to babysit him. And they'll be watching Reece, not us. There's five of us.'

'None of us is exactly in fighting trim,' I said unhappily.

'Now, don't you get your bowels in an uproar,' Earl said soothingly. 'We'll cope. And we've got one big advantage. Any one of us four could go at any time. So how many days are we putting at risk? We'd rather live high in the time we've got.'

His words were less than no comfort. 'You're carrying guns?' I asked. I already knew the answer. They avoided my eye. 'Well, for Christ's sake no shooting,' I said feebly.

156

'Not unless you can prove self-defence afterwards,' Earl said. 'Here's what we'll do. We treat it as a football play, each marking his man and coming in from the back. You, Simon, get your package off Reece and I'll back you. John marks the courier. Pete and Daniel watch out for any interference. And, listen, if you got to pull a gun, pull it first. That way there won't be any shooting and Simon can go home happy.'

Daniel and Pete exchanged a glance. 'Don't you worry, old buddy,' Pete said. 'We'll do our part.'

We distributed ourselves around the nearby shops. Earl and I looked at magazines in a shop which also catered for the smoker and the souvenir hunter. I felt more and more apprehensive. To my overtaut nerves it seemed that the elderly and infirm – and one coward – were about to take on the Mafia. I began to fear that my sphincter would let me down.

Earl was deep in a shooting magazine when something caught my eye. 'Somebody else is looking the place over,' I said. 'It's the big man in the raincoat who searched Reece's unit.' I could see him better this time, across the well-lit void. He had a battered face and cold eyes.

'Pete's seen him,' Earl said without looking up. 'Stay out of sight. He's on his own, I guess.'

At eleven twenty-eight, a middle-aged woman came up one of the escalators and walked to a position leaning against the atrium railing. John strolled past and stopped to lean over and watch the skaters below. She moved away from him.

There was still no sign of Reece. 'He's chickened out,' I said. 'We should have followed him.'

'And blown the whole thing,' Earl said. 'Hold on. Here he comes.'

Reece appeared up another escalator and walked along the gallery. He looked around. The woman nodded and he moved to join her, smirking with conscious charm.

I put my magazine back in the rack. 'Not yet,' Earl said. 'Wait until your package is out in the open. We can't take time out to search him.'

Reece and the woman exchanged a few words. She handed him some papers which he skimmed through and stuffed into a pocket. The man in the raincoat was watching from thirty yards off. I was sure now that his role was merely to observe, but I saw Daniel and Pete moving up on either side of him. There was no sign of their usual ebullience. They looked calm and purposeful.

Reece dipped into another pocket.

'Let's go,' Earl said. 'Follow a few yards behind me.'

He started out of the shop.

As Reece's hand came out of his pocket with a small but heavy package, his eyes flicked once again around the gallery. Seven pairs of eyes were on him and although no guns were in sight there is no mistaking the attitude of a man who is holding himself ready for a hurried draw.

I saw Reece's body stiffen and his face change. Earl was less than halfway towards him and I was still in the shop doorway when Reece darted suddenly towards the corner of the gallery. The woman shouted something.

Earl was too far away. Pete was quick but the man in the raincoat was faster and as light as a cat.

If I had had time to think I would have lost my nerve. But I had been fondling a smooth, round pebble as a soothing toy. I found that my other hand had produced the catapult without conscious decision on my part, and the pebble seemed to settle into the leather of its own accord.

As I drew back the rubber I looked at Reece and then decided on the man in the raincoat. But, as I let fly, Reece swung his arm and threw the package. The movement brought him into my line of fire. The pebble caught him on the temple, with a sound which I am still trying hard to forget.

His legs still ran although I think that he was out on his feet. He never completed the curve which would have taken him round the corner of the gallery and towards the head of the escalators. Instead, his run straightened and two more paces brought him up against the railing with a force which folded him over it. Next moment, he was out and falling. He never cried out, not until he hit the ice. Then there came a single shout as the air was bounced out of his lungs.

Appalled, I looked around. But nobody seemed to be paying any attention to me. The few bystanders were rushing to the railing. I moved after them.

The man in the raincoat had checked and I saw Daniel come up beside him and whisper a few words. The woman turned and walked rapidly away.

I came to the railing beside where Earl was looking down and looked for myself. Reece's body was spreadeagled on the ice, sixty feet below us. The ice had shattered, cracks radiating from the body to the edges of the rink, and fallen skaters were only now picking themselves up and moving cautiously towards the body. John must have got off his mark like a sprinter, at great risk to his heart. He was already below, moving out onto the ice, and I heard his voice say something about being a doctor.

Earl turned and grabbed my arm. 'Come,' he said. 'Quickly.'

I wanted to protest, but he was towing me along at a pace which boded ill for his quadruple bypass. 'A woman grabbed up that package,' he said. 'A blonde, looked soft enough to spread on your toast. Must've been the cunt he phoned. She's headed towards the car park. And if you want another reason, the girl in the shop saw you waste Reece. In about an hour and a half, she'll make up her mind to do something about it. For the moment she doesn't believe what she saw.'

We hurried down and through and along and up and collected Earl's car from the multi-storey car park. He took it down the ramp in a hurry and stopped in the street.

'She's away,' I said.

'We're not dead yet,' Earl said. 'Worst comes to the worst, we can—'

Pete appeared at Earl's window. For the first time, he was grinning all over his wrinkled face. 'She's in a red sports car,' he said. 'Went straight on and then made a right.'

He grabbed for the rear door handle but missed it as Earl accelerated away.

I must have closed my eyes for a few seconds while Earl threw the big car through the traffic, because I only remember the sound of tyres and being swung around as he circled an interchange.

'Got her!' he said. 'Red sports car half a mile ahead.'

We were on another dual carriageway. I seemed to have left my sense of direction behind somewhere in the Westin Galleria, but I thought that it was the Lyndon Johnson Freeway. As my eyes picked up the red sports car far ahead, it vanished around a curve. Earl's car was flat out, slicing dangerously through the traffic, but when we spotted the red car again we had hardly gained any ground. Another mile went by in a blur. Then brake-lights flared and the sports car turned off.

Earl got to the junction as quickly as the car could carry us and made the turn with more protestation from the tyres. We saw the blonde ahead make another turn. Earl slowed and cruised around a small circuit of streets. The houses were modest, medium-priced, each with an attached garage.

'Lost her,' he said. 'Guess we'll have to start again with friend Cullingpepper after all. That's if she knows about him. She may start looking for a market of her own.'

'It shouldn't be impossible to find out who's got a red sports car around here,' I said.

160

He pulled in to the side and parked. 'We can't go looking in garages,' he said. 'Not without some dumbo screaming for the cops. And we haven't time to keep watch. I want you out of here. If you get taken in for killing Reece, that'll really be a fuckup.'

'We could ask a neighbour,' I suggested.

'They'd think she'd been in an accident and we were looking for money,' he said. 'And who snitches on a blonde in a red sports car?'

'Another woman?'

'Don't count on it. If we get this wrong, she's up and running.'

Some of the mailboxes had names on them. I was calming down now. We had so nearly had the package in our hands that I was damned if I was quitting without a struggle. For the first time, my brain slipped into gear. 'Hang on,' I said. 'Let me at my luggage.'

Earl had to unlock the rear door. I got the little monitor out of my bag. The tape recorder was battery operated. When we ran it through slowly and counted the clicks we managed to piece together the phone number which Reece had called from the motel. I gave Earl half the photographs of Reece's notebook and we tried to match numbers. I was on the point of giving up when Earl gave a small whoop of triumph.

'Our luck's in,' he said. 'It's on the page of Zees.' He set the car in motion again.

'She may not have her name on the box,' I pointed out.

'Doesn't matter. We can ask a neighbour now. Looking for a friend with a red sports car. Can't remember her name but it starts with a Zee. That doesn't sound like a traffic accident.'

'It sounds more like a one night stand,' I said.

Earl was crawling while reading mailboxes. 'Eastman,' he said. 'Crawley. Hey, Zuckerman! How's about that?'

161

'Go round the block,' I said. 'See if there are any more Zeds.'

We circled round without spotting any more Zs, but I counted ten houses without a name on the door or the mailbox. Earl stopped again near the Zuckerman house. The street was quiet. There was nobody in sight to pay us any attention. The house looked dead. The garage door was down. 'Statistically,' he said, 'this has to be it.'

'According to Sod's Law,' I retorted, 'every house without a name on it has to belong to a Zutz or a Zimmerman. But it's our best bet.'

'It's our only bet,' Earl said. 'The cops could be closing in from one side and the buyers from the other. Let's give it a go. You take the back in case she tries to run out on us.'

The house was on the corner, so I had no difficulty in reaching the back door. There was no sound within the house except the ringing as Earl leaned on the doorbell. I was hidden from view by a corner of the garage and a large bush of escallonia. Riding on an adrenalin high, I had already overshot all my usual constraints and one more antisocial act would be lost beside Reece's death. I put my elbow through a small pane of glass. The fragments fell on a mat, making little sound, and I fumbled for the lock.

Earl was still ringing when I opened the door. 'The place feels empty,' I said. 'It has the smell of a house which has been empty for some time. Somebody's been wearing a powerful scent in here, but not for several hours. I think we're in the wrong house. Either that or she hasn't come home.'

He pulled the door shut. 'We'll look around anyway,' he said. 'It may not be her scent; could be the coloured maid's. She could have come home and gone out again.'

But there was an internal door to the garage and, when we looked inside, the concrete floor was barren.

162

'We made our play and we lost,' Earl said dejectedly. 'Let's get out of here before some angry householder shows up and starts shooting.'

We reached the front door in time to hear the sound of a small car pulling up and when we ducked into the tidy living room we could see a red sports car in front of the garage.

She came straight into the living room and from either side of the door we grabbed her arms. She turned out to be a synthetic blonde with a face which had been around longer than a first glance suggested but a figure which, although ample, was very good. From my glimpse before I put my hand over her mouth, her features suggested a gentleness which would have been wasted on Dave Reece.

Her surprise and fear were such that she lost control and broke wind loudly. 'Don't make another sound,' I said. It came to me that I could have expressed myself with more tact.

Earl passed me her other arm and I held both her wrists in one hand, still covering her mouth with the other while Earl opened the large handbag on her arm.

'Nothing,' he said. Behind the lady's back he pulled a face and fanned the air. I knew what he meant. Her flatulence, combining with a less than delicate perfume, was beginning to make my eyes water.

'Is there a receipt in there?' I asked. 'Bank or post office?'

'Nope.' He shifted his feet uncomfortably. 'You want to search her?'

I was sure that the figure shuddering gently against me was not hiding anything hard and heavy. 'Not a lot,' I said.

'You?'

He glanced at the thin dress and shook his head. 'No point,' he said. 'She was dropping it off somewhere. There's shops and a post office on the corner. Or she could have another friend. Where is it, honey?'

I uncovered her mouth. She was too scared to scream but she had a reserve of courage left. 'Don't know what you're talking about,' she whispered.

'You know,' I said. 'And you know Dave Reece is dead. Nobody ever survived a fall like that. These people play rough.' There seemed to be no harm giving the opposition the credit for my deed. 'We're from the real owners. Give it back before you get hurt. Otherwise, you'll never see a penny.'

She pursed her lips and said nothing.

'Now you listen to me,' Earl said sternly. 'You'll be watched from here on. If you look for a buyer, we'll know. And you're as likely to make contact with the same guys, who'd just as soon grab it for nothing. Give it to us and there'll be a reward. Not as much as Reece was asking, but look where he is now.'

She looked from one to the other of us and shook her head again.

The telephone started to ring. It was all that was needed to remind us that our time might be running out.

We left her tied by the thumbs to a door handle with parcel string and got out of there, breathing deeply. Earl almost pushed me into the car and set off again in a hurry.

'People!' he said. 'I guess God should have stopped at something he did well, like monkeys. Did you ever smell anything worse?'

'Never. Where now?' I asked.

'Airport. You can still catch the B-Cal plane if there's a seat left. I want you out of here.'

'What about you?'

'Hell, I didn't knock anybody over with a slingshot. Worst anybody can say I did was to bust in on Mz Zuckerman. And she won't be pressing any charges, not just for that. That's why I didn't accept your kind invite to search her. Could've been fun, though.'

164

'Can you keep watch on her?'

'We'll try. But for the moment she isn't believing that her lover's dead. When that sinks in, she'll be shit-scared. Also, she reckons that as long as she's the only person knows where it is, nobody's going to knock her off. She won't go near the stuff for a year at least. If Keith's lucky, his secrets will be obsolete before they see the light of day again. I guess we'll give her a few days to recover and then have somebody phone her. He represents Winchester or Remington, somebody too big to have to play rough. He's ready to pay her off just to prevent Keith's new load competing with their product. Keith can tell me how high he's prepared to go.'

He made another turn. I recognised the road. We were nearing the airport.

'You'll phone Keith for me?'

'I'll do that,' he said.

'He'll be in touch. He'll want to settle up with you.'

'He can forget it,' Earl said. 'Hell, you paid most of the bills. We'd have spent more than we did, just keeping ourselves amused. Tell Keith I'm sorry we lost out and all we want's an invitation to shoot your red grouse some time. I hear that they're real tricky.'

It seemed to me that grouse were about to go out of season. 'It won't be until next August,' I said.

'Whenever. There's no rush. All we've got is time. Then we'll see if you're as good with a shotgun as you are with a slingshot.'

At the terminal he parked on some forbidding looking lines. I got my bag out of the back. 'Don't forget this!' He hung something over my shoulder. 'The gun the fuss was all about, for God's sake!'

The terminal was crowded. Earl knew the way. Moving at his deceptive pace, he carved a route for me towards the British Caledonian desk. Even among Texans he was large and a path seemed to open for him.

An hour later, I was boarding the plane. As I took my seat, a British Caledonian stewardess was stowing something in the overhead locker. Her elbow dislodged the Dallas Gun Club cap which I had forgotten that I was wearing.

She picked it up for me. 'I'm so sorry,' she said.

After the days spent talking with Earl and his friends, the proper response jumped onto my tongue. 'It don't make a shit, ma'am,' I said.

She turned away to one of her colleagues. 'Another damned Texan,' she said under her breath.

ELEVEN

On the flight back I began to wind down slowly and even
came to terms with the fact that I had killed Dave Reece.
Illogically, the fact that I had instead intended to kill, or at
least to maim, the man in the raincoat helped me by making
my action seem less deliberate. I think that I slept a little.
We landed at Gatwick at what had somehow become seven
the next morning. Keith was waiting for me in Customs.

'What are you doing here?' I asked.

'Making sure you don't end up in the shairn,' he said.
Shairn, I knew, was Scots for cow-dung.

'Why would I?'

'You're a British national. You can't come waltzing into
the country with a shotgun and no certificate. But you can
deliver it to me, as a licensed dealer. I came down on the
last shuttle last night and dozed in a chair in the lounge.'

He had gone to some trouble on my behalf but I was
rather off Keith at that moment. 'Just to get your hands
on Sir Philip's gun?' I asked.

'You'll get the reward,' he said sourly. 'You can pay my
fare out of it.'

If I had succeeded in his other errand I would have told
him to pay his own damn fare. 'I'll reimburse you,' I said.
'But I think you've got a bloody nerve.'

'You too. And you look like hell.'

I knew what he meant. I was beardless but had again
forgotten to shave. We were both tired and fed up.

The departure lounge for the shuttle looked squalid by Dallas standards. We managed a quick cup of revolting coffee.

During the flight to Turnhouse and again in his car, he questioned me closely about all that I had seen, done, heard, thought, felt and imagined while in Texas. Some of his questions had me puzzled. In the car, which still showed crumpled bodywork but seemed to be in running order, I played him the tapes of Reece's phone calls, several times, but before I could ask what he made of them I noticed that we were not on the shortest route around Edinburgh.

'I want to get home and to bed,' I said.

'This won't take long. I played that tape over the phone to Charlie,' Keith said, 'and he phoned Cathcart and asked him to trace the phone number. Yesterday, he called Charlie back and asked him how he got the number. Charlie said that our agent in the States was hot on Reece's trail and that Reece seemed to have phoned that number.

'Cathcart hummed and hawed and Charlie told him that he wasn't playing fair. In the end, Cathcart said this much. The number belonged to a house occupied by a woman. From what a neighbour told the police, a man who could have been Reece had been there most nights for the past few months.'

I was too tired to get excited about it. 'Have you been to see her?' I asked idly.

'Cathcart wouldn't cough up the address and he said that she'd died in an accident, early on Sunday morning. He said that the Lothians force were investigating and they were taking it seriously because she'd been mixing with a tough crowd. If we poked our noses in, the whole story would come out.'

'Dead end,' I said.

'It was. Then it occurred to me to look in the local paper.' Keith pulled in to the roadside. He handed me a cutting from a newspaper. I read it while he consulted a street map.

168

GAS BLAST KILLS WIDOW

Mrs Sheila Conran (32) was killed outright when a blast shattered her home early yesterday morning. Mrs Conran, a widow, is believed to have just returned from her work at a gaming club in central Edinburgh when . . .

The remainder of the story added few details but was padded with uninformative comments from the Gas Board, the police and several neighbours. On reading the story for the third time I pointed out that the address was not mentioned.

'That hit me in the eye,' Keith said. He put the map away and pulled out into the traffic. 'But among the S. Conrans in the phone book I found the number Reece asked for. I want to take a look at it. It's not far off our route.'

The street turned out to be one of those forgotten corners which have been left behind by the march of progress. A dozen or so run-down houses were interspersed with small workshops, a few lockup garages, some allotments and corners of derelict land so far undiscovered by the speculative builders.

There was still police activity in the street and when Keith tried to slow down he was waved on by a constable with a luminous green waistcoat over his uniform. We had seen enough.

Keith drove on and headed for home. 'If that was a gas explosion,' he said, 'Krakatoa was a careless fart.' But he seemed to put the almost demolished house out of his mind for the moment. 'Earl was right,' he said disgustedly. 'That woman had got the package hidden somewhere. And you chickened out, the pair of you!'

'It couldn't have been in the house,' I said. 'You know how a place smells different when the dust's had time to settle and the air's changed. Besides, she was wearing a perfume that made your head swim but you could only smell a trace of it in the house. So she hadn't been back. What would you have done?' I asked him. 'Torture? Kidnap?'

'At least I'd have searched her for a receipt from the bank or the post office.'

'I expect you would,' I said. 'But you wouldn't have enjoyed it. She's a bit overblown for your taste.'

He ignored my dig at him. 'And I'd have put the fear of God into her.'

'We tried that,' I said. 'That's another reason why you wouldn't have enjoyed it. I don't know why they talk about getting the wind up,' I added sleepily. 'That's not the direction it goes at all.'

'The trouble with you,' he said, unsmiling, 'is that you're too much of a gentleman and, even with you looking like that, she could see it.'

He fell silent and seemed lost in thought. I decided not to feel insulted. I dozed until we swept past the by-road to Keith's house. 'Alice went home,' he said suddenly. 'And Boss. They're both fine.'

'That's good,' I said.

'Earl says that they thought a lot of you.'

'They did?' I had had the impression that Earl and his friends had thought me a bit of a wimp. And that Keith thought the same.

'Earl wouldn't say much about what happened at the end. I gather that Dave Reece has gone to Another Place, and is no doubt by now bugging St Peter's gatehouse on behalf of the devil?'

'You could put it like that,' I said.

Keith turned out of the Square in Newton Lauder and headed out towards Tansy House. 'Earl hinted – no more than that – but he hinted that you'd had more than a finger in Reece's death. And that that's why he put you on a plane in a hurry.'

'Oh, yes?'

'Yes. He phoned again to say that his friend John managed to get the papers out of Reece's pocket. I told him to burn the cheque and any other papers and just to keep the letter, in case Cullingpepper and his friends ever tried to make trouble. Burning the cheque is as good as burning cash as far as they're concerned, so it should keep them at each other's throats until the dust's settled.'

I was realising that he had more excuse than I had for feeling out of sorts. 'I'm sorry I blew it,' I said.

His mood, like mine, had softened. 'You didn't blow it. You just didn't quite get there. You were beaten by a dead man who had thought one step too far ahead. To be honest, I never dared hope that you'd get as far as you did. You must be more on the ball than you ever let on. Oh, well! Earl thinks that the samples may never surface again. He may be right. Have breakfast and a bath and you'll feel better. And shave, unless you're going to go in for topiary again. I'll come for you later.'

'I'm going to bed. I've been on the go for twenty-eight hours straight.'

'Less six hours time difference,' he pointed out. He bit back a yawn of his own. 'I'll phone and tell you when I'm coming. Superintendent Cathcart wants to meet me at Aikhowe and he wants you along. He mentioned you by name. But unless your activities in the States could stand up to police scrutiny, say nothing about them except to answer my questions.'

'What does he want?'

'He didn't say but it sounded urgent. Bring the tapes and your photographs and so on. And give Charlie his bits and pieces back.'

'His bugs are still in place,' I said. 'I've got the rest.'

We were slowing for Tansy House. I could see Alice at the door and Boss at her feet. 'Simon,' Keith said plaintively, 'what did happen to Reece? Not a word beyond this car, I swear it.'

I decided to leave him wondering. I had no objection to accepting credit for the work of the Texans, or to Keith believing that I had committed murder on his behalf. The truth was less glamorous than Keith's mental images would be. I waited until the car had stopped and then let him see that I was hiding a quiet smile. 'I always find that it's better to let these things be forgotten,' I said.

I left him exuding frustration and went inside to face another string of questions, this time about people and places and clothes and food and weather and life, with crime at the tail end of a long list. It even continued while I was in the bath. And Boss sat beside me and panted into my ear. We were all glad that I was back.

Although the local garage had restored Keith's car to running order, Molly had made it clear that she had no intention of running around in a car which looked as if it had been rescued from a breaker's yard and she had appropriated the jeep which was not only Keith's shooting vehicle but contained most of his shooting gear.

So Keith had left the car at the garage again, for urgent attention to the bodywork, and we arrived at Aikhowe in mid-afternoon in Alice's Mini – Keith, myself, Alice who had flatly refused to be left behind and Boss who was never abandoned if it was possible to take him with us.

A police Jaguar swept past as we neared Aikhowe, almost blowing the Mini off the road, and we arrived on the gravel to find Charlie speaking on the doorstep to Superintendent Cathcart. A police sergeant and Charlie's security man were eyeing each other. They all looked at Alice in doubt but said nothing. Sometimes being an attractive girl has its advantages. Boss, locked in the car, settled down across the back seat in contentment.

Charlie led us through to his private quarters with Cathcart almost treading on his heels in impatience. A fire blazing in the grate was helping the central heating to

172

raise the room almost to Texan levels of temperature.

The Superintendent was speaking almost before we had settled ourselves on to Charlie's worn but comfortable furniture.

'Your time ran out several days ago,' he said. 'Things have moved on. We have to open up a full investigation. I'm sorry.'

'So am I,' Keith said. He glanced at Charlie and back to Cathcart. 'Our agent in America failed to recover our goods. Well, swings and roundabouts! At least it means that the time for secrecy is over. We can seek help from the Dallas police.'

Charlie, rather white in the face, looked down at the table.

'So be it,' Cathcart said. I had a feeling that he was watching me out of the corner of his eye. 'Although they may not be as much help to you as you would be to them. I asked them for word of Reece, only to be told that he'd been killed in a fall. They traced him back to a motel. I made an enquiry – very guarded, you'll be glad to hear – as to whether there was anything unusual in his luggage. Apart from some tools and electronic components, there wasn't.'

'What a pity!' Keith said. He sounded sincere. I avoided his eye.

'Manpower being in short supply,' Cathcart said, 'I had an excuse to soft-pedal the Lucas investigation while I waited for the post mortem report. And we were busy enough with a bomb scare in Glasgow. An MP had a threatening letter and every available man was called in to protect him. It turned out to be a hoax.'

'For a while, though, you thought that bombs were being made in Edinburgh,' Keith said quietly.

'We did.' Cathcart sat up straight. 'How the hell did you know that?'

'You carefully didn't give us the address for that phone number, but the papers mentioned a gas explosion. It had to be the right accident. According to the papers, the victim worked in a gaming club. That call was placed at nine p.m., their time. Who else would Reece have had a pre-arrangement to phone at what was already three in the morning over here, a time when only gamblers are still up and about? The phone directory confirmed the number and gave me the address. So I went to have a look. The gable was blown out, half the slates stripped off the roof and there were police all over the place. You thought that a bomber had blown himself or herself up by accident.'

'It's still difficult to find any other explanation,' Cathcart said. 'But our hoaxer turned out to be a disgruntled ex-employee with no intention except to make a damned nuisance of himself, so the explosion rests with Lothian and Borders and I'm back with the Donald Lucas case.'

'I wouldn't forget about the bomb just yet,' Keith said. 'What did the forensic scientists make of it?'

'Not very much,' Cathcart said. 'A home-made explosive— '

'Sodium chlorate and sugar?' Keith suggested. 'Or ammonium nitrate and oil?'

'A little more sophisticated than either of those, and much more powerful, but just as easy to obtain. Plus some home-made napalm to make sure of a good blaze.' Cathcart paused and for a moment I could see him as an old man. Then he shrugged and went on. 'Bombers are getting too clever by half,' he said briskly. 'Wiring of magnesium alloys which disappear altogether in a fire. They've found no sign of a timer. The remains of some bits which look like radio components suggest that it may have been triggered that way.'

Keith shook his head slowly.

Cathcart looked at him very hard. 'What the hell do you know about it?' he demanded.

'Did you ever see the deceased Mrs Conran?'

'I saw what was left of her.' Cathcart shivered. 'Unrecognisable.'

'You saw a photograph of her as she was before the blast?'

'No.'

'I think you did,' Keith said. 'In Donald Lucas's cottage. She was his new girlfriend.'

Cathcart stared at him and then looked around Charlie's drawing room. 'Where's your telephone?' he demanded.

Charlie pointed to a telephone behind the Superintendent's back, on the table where the Sergeant was taking notes. 'Or you can be more private in the hall,' he said.

Cathcart displaced his subordinate and dialled a number from memory. He held a short conversation with somebody whom he addressed as Ian and came back to his chair. 'From the descriptions which they got from the neighbours, it's possible. But, assuming that you're right, how did you guess?'

Instead of answering, Keith turned to me. 'I never met Reece, Simon, but you did. What did you make of him?'

'An arrogant, handsome bastard,' I said. 'From what I saw of him, he fell within the classic definition of a psychopath, in that he didn't believe that any laws of God or man applied to him.'

'Would he hesitate to kill, to cover his tracks?'

'Not for an instant,' I said.

'Blind guesswork,' Cathcart said triumphantly. 'Just for once you were right, but for the wrong reason. Reece didn't kill Donald Lucas.'

'I never said that he did,' Keith pointed out, 'only, some days ago, that he seemed a likely suspect. I suppose that the pathologist's report on Donald Lucas fixed the time of death? They don't usually,' he added.

'We had a stroke of luck,' Cathcart admitted. 'We can't be unlucky all the time.'

'Just most of it?'

'You're not wrong. At first, nobody at the hotel was sure at what time he left there. According to the pathologist's report, Lucas had eaten a ham roll and washed it down with a glass of shandy about an hour before he died. So we went back to the hotel. The waitress suddenly remembered him taking just such a snack around six p.m. on the Tuesday. At which time, Reece was already in Aberdeen and waiting for his plane.'

'I thought as much,' Keith said. He turned to me again. 'Would you say that Reece was the type who could charm women into doing his dirty work for him?'

Remembering the phone calls, I said that he was.

'There you are,' Keith told Cathcart. 'I never liked your idea of Reece holding a gun on Lucas and forcing him to drink vodka. Any beggar as thrawn and suspicious as myself would guess what he was up to and say, "Fuck you! Kill me if you want, but I'm not making it easy for you to get away with it."'

'How much easier for a girlfriend to say, "We're going to be rich and I've decided to accept your proposition and come away with you and I'll be very hurt if you don't join me in a drink to seal the bargain." Lucas had an idiosyncrasy. It took very little alcohol to knock him out. I know that a vodka bottle was found in the car, but what was in his stomach?'

'Vodka mixed with beer,' Cathcart said. 'Certainly not enough vodka to account for a nearly empty bottle – if the bottle was full to start off with. But I'll give you this much – if he had such an idiosyncrasy, a girlfriend would have been the first to know about it. He may not even have known that he was drinking spirits.' He looked at his watch. He was always a man in a hurry. 'Now, I've said rather more than I came to say. It's time for you to cough up anything you know. And then I must go and set the wheels in motion.'

Keith is not usually forthcoming with the police, but he surprised me by nodding vigorously. 'Let's run through it chronologically,' he said.

Charlie, who had been sitting slumped, brooding over the inevitability of disaster to his reputation, looked up. 'Good idea,' he said. 'If we must expose our sores, at least let's stop leaping about in time and getting into arguments because all the facts aren't out yet. I suppose it's up to me to set the ball rolling.

'David Reece was a professional industrial spy who walked out of the comparatively respectable agency where he worked and set up in business for himself last summer. His motivation seems to have been that he was paid by results and he felt that he couldn't get results within the rules laid down by the firm. He was a skilled investigator and technician, and absolutely ruthless.

'He decided that my organisation would be a profitable field for study. At that time, because of legislation impending world-wide, the market was becoming ripe for a whole new approach to the shotgun cartridge and we were bringing together some Swedish research, a British plastics manufacturer and several cartridge makers to develop and market a basic idea of Keith's.'

Keith recognised Charlie's glance as a signal to take over. 'But,' he said, 'Charlie's – Lord Jedburgh's – security is thorough. Reece needed an insider, at least to tell him what to go after. He could hardly approach the staff, one at a time, rustling a fistful of fivers and whispering, "There's another million where this came from." As Simon confirmed, Reece was a man of powerful sex appeal and he seems to have been ready to use it. So he did what he and others had done before, found an attractive girl of low character and brought her under his spell. No doubt he suggested that her task was a one-off, aimed at setting the pair of them up for life in some paradise. And she attached herself to poor Donald Lucas, feeding him a similar line of bull. Lucas was vulnerable and he fell heavily.'

'I feel bad about Donald,' Charlie said. 'As his employer, I should have seen what he was going through. But who could guess, when the only symptom which he showed was contentment?

'Donald was our expert on patent law. So he could get his hands on our papers but without understanding the technicalities. I think that that part of the paperwork which might have been of use to Reece went through Donald's hands well before Reece and he got together. And I make damned sure that nobody has access to any papers which he does not need at that time. Which, of course, is why the only photocopiers in the place are visible from my office. So on its own what Donald knew or could supply was relatively useless.

'It happened, however, that we were due to send samples to a large Italian manufacturer. We had reason to believe that Reece had managed to interfere with the mails. But it also happened that Donald was due to send a pair of his trained Dobermanns to Italy. In a moment of aberration – which I'll admit was my fault and which in retrospect looks crazy – we decided to send the samples to Italy in the dogs' travelling boxes, with a guard to watch over the dogs.'

'Ingenious,' the Superintendent said. He laughed suddenly. 'What I'd have done would have been to seal the stuff up in a large bone. I wouldn't fancy anybody's chances of taking a bone away from a trained Dobermann.' He chuckled again at this quaint flight of imagination.

Keith and Charlie locked eyes.

Charlie sighed deeply. 'This is in confidence,' he said. 'My organisation may survive looking incompetent, but never looking funny. We did exactly as you just said.'

Cathcart, again the responsible and humourless policeman, kept a straight face. But as Charlie and I unfolded between us the story of the bones, and of Boss's part in their adventures, he broke down and laughed until tears hopped down his cheeks. He sobered suddenly when I came to my encounter with Reece at the roadside. 'This should have been reported.'

'But not to you,' Keith pointed out. 'Nor would it have helped. Reece was out of the country long before you could have caught up with him. He had only hung around, trying to borrow the dog again, because he wasn't sure whether the package he had was the real one or the dummy. By mischance, Simon uttered some words which gave him the idea of opening up one of the ordinary cartridges in his possession. That's how some pellets got spilled in the car he was using. When he saw that the shot and the wad bore little or no resemblance to those in the stolen package, he knew that he was already on a winner. He'd had what he wanted all the time.

'The girl's job, apart from winkling out the information and persuading Donald Lucas to co-operate, was to keep him out of the way until the goods were out of the country. She had taken a few days off her work at the gaming club—'

'She phoned in to say that she was ill,' the Superintendent said.

'And she stayed with Lucas at the Greenmilns Inn,' Keith resumed, 'conveniently forgetting to post his card to his employer. But here, Superintendent, you may be able to fill a gap. Between Newton Lauder and Aberdeen, Reece must have met up with Mrs Conran. The times don't allow for his doing a circular tour of Scotland.'

'You're guessing a lot,' Cathcart said, 'but your guesses seem to be near the truth. You're thinking of the sweater which was used in the fake suicide?'

'That's just what,' Keith said.

'I thought as much. Forensic said that it had been worn by a red-haired man. According to the hotel receptionist

179

Mrs Lucas, as she knew her, got a phone call at around noon on the Tuesday. She left Lucas to cool his heels for the afternoon. She could have met Reece somewhere on his route.'

Keith nodded. 'We had word of a possible sighting of Reece in Perth,' he said.

'Go on guessing,' said Cathcart. 'You can leave me to prove or disprove your guesses later.'

Keith nodded again, more slowly. I was thinking through a layer of treacle but, although he must have been as tired as I was, I could see that Keith's mind was racing ahead. 'So they met. Probably, Reece had delayed until the latest possible minute before telling the girl about the last part of her job. From what we know about Reece, he was both thorough and ruthless.

'Donald Lucas could still undo all the good work. He was expecting his reward from the woman – who, it can be assumed, had every intention of dropping him as soon as Reece beckoned – and when the promised life of love and nooky failed to mature he would blow his stack.

'Now, take note of this. Evidence of an illicit sale of the secret, from Lucas or the girl, could render it worthless by tying it up in litigation until others had grabbed hold of the market. Lucas had to die. Reece needed a personal meeting with the girl to put this across. He explained exactly what she had to do. He probably provided the tube and the vodka. He certainly gave her a sweater with which to stuff up the gap over the window. And he promised that if she would do this one little thing for him they would go off into the sunset together and live happily ever after.'

'Exactly what Mrs Conran would have said to Donald Lucas,' Cathcart said. 'The most you can say about Reece is that he was consistent in his evil.'

'He remained consistent,' Keith said. 'Superintendent, we have only just started on Reece. Mrs Conran, in her turn, was a potential embarrassment to him. If he failed to come back for her, she was going to be in the classic position of a woman scorned. It would be a toss-up whether her fear of a murder charge would outweigh her desire to get back at her faithless lover by telling the whole world about stolen secrets. Reece knew this from the beginning. And he was not the man to risk it.

'While he was living in her house, he planted his bomb. It was linked to the telephone. And when he phoned her from the States at a pre-arranged time, nine p.m. Central Standard Time and three a.m. by ours, she answered the phone with the code-word which told him that all was well. Without even bothering to say a word, he sent the signal which triggered the device.'

The recording of Reece's phone call to Scotland had been transferred to a separate cassette. Charlie played it. Cathcart listened to the short burst of electronic noise and his eyebrows went up. 'That could trigger a bomb?' he asked incredulously.

'Without any difficulty,' Charlie said. 'You'd need little more than matching microchips. The one at the receiving end recognises the signal, passes a tiny current, a relay closes and a much larger current fires a detonator.'

'And that's about all that we have to tell you,' Keith said.

Cathcart got out of his chair. He walked the length of the big room and back while he thought. He stopped beside his Sergeant. 'You've got all that down?'

The Sergeant nodded. 'Sir,' he said.

Cathcart moved to the Adam fireplace and leaned on the mantel. 'It all fits together,' he said suddenly. 'And it fits all the evidence we've got so far. I must go. The Bomb Squad can re-examine the remains from the Conran house and we can do a more thorough check into the movements of Reece and Lucas and the girl. Forensic may turn up some more evidence, now that we know what we're looking for.'

Keith had seen my photographs. 'Tell the Dallas police to look again through Reece's things,' he said. 'They'll

181

probably find the electronic gubbins – and a cassette player, if he'd transferred the electronic noise to tape.'

Charlie's quick mind had already absorbed the shift of circumstances and was rushing ahead. 'So I don't get my car back for another few weeks,' he said.

'That's right. But,' Cathcart said, 'look on the bright side, my lord. If the whole story checks out, the participants are dead. With no prosecution to come, publicity can be kept to the minimum. And now I must get going. The taking of statements can wait.' He got to his feet and looked down at me from his considerable height. 'You seem to have removed your beard, Mr Parbitter. I hear some strange stories from Dallas. But, luckily for you, that's a long way off my patch and the Dallas police have not asked for our help. Let's hope that nothing changes. No need to see us out, my lord. Sergeant.'

When the policemen were out of the room we all began to speak at once. Keith and Charlie were deep in argument as to whether the questionable advantage of enlisting the Dallas police to recover the samples outweighed Charlie's concern about publicity, while I was demanding to know whether such a move would bring me to the attention of any police force, anywhere.

Alice stirred in her chair. She had been so quiet that we had forgotten her. She spoke softly, but there was something in her tones which cut through the other voices. 'Now that they've gone,' she said, 'can I say something? I think it's urgent,' she added uncertainly.

TWELVE

Alice is very easy to look at. Our stares seemed to throw her into confusion. Unusually for a woman, she never likes to be the object of male gaze. 'What you said about Dave Reece,' she said, blushing. 'His character. His evil. His consistency. I don't think you've thought it right through.'

'Probably not,' Keith said. 'We haven't had it for very long.'

'I think maybe you've taken too long already,' Alice said. 'Simon told me a little about the phone calls. I wondered about the Sunday evening one. The one from the woman. That wasn't the same person he phoned two days later?'

'I assumed that it was,' I said. 'I didn't notice any difference between the voices. But, thinking it over, he wouldn't have let her go off to Florida for a few days if she was holding his package and he was expecting to do a deal.'

'Unless he had access to her house,' Keith said.

'Could we . . . ' Alice paused. She always felt herself to be an intruder in such discussions although her suggestions were never far from the point. 'Please, would you play the tape of that call?'

'Of course.' Charlie said. He still had his cassette player beside him. I took the cassette out of my pocket and we listened in silence to the recording.

When it was finished, Keith called on the Almighty in terms which that Being would certainly not have appreciated. 'We've been stupid,' he said. 'Blind stupid. What was the Zuckerman woman's number?'

I still had my note of it. Keith had moved to the telephone. He was dialling even as I read the number out. He looked at Alice as the exchanges took over. 'You'd better speak,' he said. 'A man's voice might panic her.'

Alice sat at the phone and took the receiver. 'It's not ringing,' she said. 'If the other woman's back from Florida already . . . '

'Dial again,' Keith said. He sounded choked.

I felt the sweat cold on my back. Reece's words were still in my ears. *If it's over and it's gone bad, if I've been crossed up, there's one person could have set me up and that person knows too much to go on walking around. You'll know what to do about that? And the woman's reply. It'll be a pleasure. The thing I've got here?*

Keith was right. We had been stupid. More precisely, I had been stupid. The evidence had been in my hands but I had been blind. If the other woman, who may or may not have been Reece's 'one for real', had returned from Florida . . .

She had not. 'It's ringing,' Alice said. I think that we gave a small cheer.

Keith had been speaking to Charlie. 'The hall in the phone's on another line,' Charlie gabbled. The anxiety was getting to him also.

'Come through,' Keith said to me.

'There's no answer,' Alice said.

I did a little mental arithmetic. 'She can't still be asleep,' I said. 'Not unless she's another croupier. Maybe she's out.'

In the hall, Keith grabbed up the phone. 'Which of Earl's pals lives nearest to Dallas?'

'I think John lives at Greenville,' I said. 'That's only about forty minutes by car. But I don't have a number.'

'Goddam! Maybe Earl's left another message on his answering machine,' Keith said. He started dialling.

I moved back to the doorway. Alice's voice came through suddenly, breathless with relief. 'Mrs Zuckerman? Oh, Miss Zuckerman. I'm calling from Scotland. Yes, Scotland Europe. Please don't panic and for God's sake don't hang up the phone . . . '

Then Keith's voice from the other side. 'Earl? Thank God you're at home. Don't talk yet, just listen. Which of your pals is nearest Dallas? Daniel? The gadget fiend? He's still in Dallas? You think he could disconnect a bomb from a telephone line? Phone him . . . '

I tuned in to Alice again. 'No, it isn't a trick to get you out of the house. Stay there if you want. What can you lose? You're perfectly safe as long as you don't hang up the phone.' I bent and whispered into her spare ear. She relayed the message. 'My friends – the real owners of the parcel you've been holding – are arranging for somebody to come and disconnect it. Yes, at once. He won't do anything else, just disconnect it.'

Keith joined me in the doorway. 'Earl's sending Daniel. It should be safe enough. Reece had no reason to fit booby-traps. Earl will call back here when they know more.'

'My dear,' Alice was saying, 'Dave Reece was only using you. And I'm afraid you're not the first he's used and then planned to kill. He seems to have been a very bad man. It won't be easy but you must try to forget him . . . '

'My God!' Charlie said. 'Alice isn't planning to keep her talking until Earl's friend gets there, is she?'

'Probably,' I said.

The phone rang in the hall. Keith darted to answer it.

'My friend – Lord Jedburgh – is getting anxious about his phone bill,' Alice said. 'Yes, he's a real lord. An earl, no less. I'll have to ring off now. But, remember, you're quite safe as long as you don't hang up the phone. What?' She listened for a moment and then turned to Charlie, smiling her shy smile. 'She wants to talk to you. She never spoke with a real lord before.'

Keith finished speaking in the hall and came back to me. 'That was Earl,' he said. 'The other Earl. Daniel's on his way. Earl says he's delighted to have the activity. And he says that the Dallas police think the girl in the shop had been smoking something which made her dream dreams, whatever he means by that. So they're not looking for you. They've written Reece's death off as an accident. But don't come back yet awhile.' He gave me his grim, determined look. 'Some day you're going to tell me exactly what happened.'

'Don't hold your breath,' I said.

Charlie had managed to finish his conversation with the distant Miss Zuckerman. He looked at his watch. 'My housekeeper's gone home by now,' he said. 'I'll see if I can rustle up something to eat.'

Charlie's idea of 'rustling up something to eat' took an hour. While we waited, we managed to sustain only disjointed conversation. Each of our minds was on other things.

At last, Charlie produced steaks with three vegetables, fruit, cheese and two bottles of a modest wine. Hunger immediately rushed over me again, but we had hardly started to eat when the phone in the hall began to ring. A stillness settled on us.

'You go,' Charlie said to Keith. 'It'll be your friend Earl.'

Keith nodded and left the room in a hurry. I found that I was haunted by a vision of the kindly Daniel, silenced more completely and for ever, blown to the winds.

We picked at our food until Keith came back. He was looking very solemn. 'That was Earl,' he said. 'He's just got the news. Daniel disconnected the device safely and is on the way to Lake Ray Hubbard to get rid of it.' His face broke up suddenly into a huge grin. 'And it seems that Miss Zuckerman was overcome with the realisation of the rough company she'd been mixing with. Between that and noble lords, Daniel only had to fondle the device and drop a few hints and she coughed up our package into his hot little hands. Whee!' Keith looked as if he were thinking about turning a handspring, but he thought better of it.

'Marvellous!' Charlie said. He seemed undecided whether to laugh or weep.

'He promised her a thousand dollars and a trip to Europe,' Keith said, 'which seems little enough in the circumstances.' He resumed his seat and began work on his steak. 'I'll tell you something else,' he said with his mouth full. 'When the device was disconnected, they hung up the phone. It rang again immediately. She picked it up. And only a loud bleep came over the line.'

Charlie got up and gathered his two wine bottles. 'I'll get rid of this muck,' he said. 'I think we can find something better to celebrate with. My old man left a few bottles behind him.'

'That's not all,' Keith said. 'They're coming over, the four of them, bringing our goodies with them. They say that if it's too late for grouse, a day at the pheasants will do them. Perhaps they'll bring Miss Zuckerman along. She seemed very taken with your noble lordship.'

'Let her come. I'll give them a day here,' Charlie said. 'Just the six of us. Simon and Boss can come and pick up again.'

'I think we can find them something better than that as a reward,' Keith said. 'You've only got about ten birds left on the ground. I'll see what I can fix.' He pinned the young Earl with a stony eye. 'And you can bloody well pay for it, Charlie,' he said. 'You and your bloody bones!'

'I'll even do that,' Charlie said. He went out to fetch his wine.

187

Keith was looking at me. He swallowed a large mouthful. 'Earl said one more thing. He said that Daniel seemed very taken with Miss Zuckerman. He said that he guessed that Daniel had gotten more than one wish. What the hell would that mean?'

'No idea,' I said. But, thinking back, I remembered something. Daniel had told us that he would have swapped Sir Philip's Purdey for just one erection.

THIRTEEN

Sir Philip Dunne arrived on our doorstep next morning. He was in an ebullient mood. 'My boy!' he said. 'My dear boy! Young Charlie tells me you've worked the magic. He tells me that I mustn't ask questions, but . . . Dallas, of all places, I believe?'

'That's right,' I said dully. I was still hung over from Charlie's party. This had grown and grown as we were joined by members of his staff who, although not allowed to know any details, were aware that there was cause for celebration. A car had been sent for Bill Haddo. The radio ham had proved to be the life of the party, with a fund of technical anecdotes suited to the company and an incredible thirst for whisky. As he pointed out, to be drunk in charge of a wheelchair was not yet a crime. Towards three in the morning, Dr Prestatyn had been reciting Rabbie Burns . . .

'I've been there often,' Sir Philip said. 'Is Ninfa's still in business?'

I assured him that it was, took him in and gave him a seat. Alice joined us. She had drunk very little but nevertheless I was amazed at how fresh and bright she looked after such a night.

'Mrs Parbitter!' Sir Philip exclaimed, rising stiffly. 'I was just about to congratulate your husband.'

Alice winked at me. I knew what she was thinking. 'He did very well, didn't he?' she said. 'I knew that he could write about cloaks and daggers, but I never realised that he could live them. Do sit down. We've been discussing how to spend the reward.'

Sir Philip's exuberance dimmed and the natural redness of his face paled slightly. 'Ah yes. The reward. Five hundred, wasn't it?'

'It was five thousand,' Alice said firmly, 'and you know it. We both heard it and so did Mr Calder.'

Under Scots law, a contract is dangerously easy to establish as Sir Philip was well aware. His face took on the look of one who has just passed the Flymo over a dog-turd. 'But that's excessive. If I ever mentioned such a sum, it was in the belief that a great deal of time and trouble would be involved.'

'He had to follow it to the States,' Alice said reproachfully. 'Really, Sir Philip, I'm surprised that somebody in your position . . . '

'I no longer have a position,' Sir Philip broke in. If he felt a temptation to refer to himself as a poor old pensioner, he managed to resist it. 'I am retired. Charlie admitted that your husband was over there for some other reason. And it's barely a week since I asked for his help. Come along, now,' he said reasonably. 'After all, five hundred is still a lot of money.'

I sighed. 'At least we could get a holiday out of it,' I said feebly.

'We don't need holidays,' Alice snapped. 'It's high time we had a decent car and five hundred won't look at it. Simon dear, go and write something. I'll deal with this.'

I did as I was told with relief. Alice should have been the one to go to the States. She can show a streak of firmness which I could never match. I soon sank myself in the intricacies of the plot for a novel. Raised voices from the living room and the eventual slamming of doors barely reached my consciousness. I came to when Alice tiptoed into the study and stood quietly at my elbow. She never realises that she could as well be preceded by a pipe band without distracting me any more completely.

'Well, hello,' I said mildly. She put down a cheque in front of me. I looked at it. It said Five Thousand Pounds. 'How on earth did you manage that?' I asked.

She giggled. 'I fetched his gun out and put it down across two chairs and I threatened to sit down hard on the middle of it and bounce up and down until I'd bent it into a hoop if he didn't honour his word. He's so stiff these days that I could have got in ten bounces before he even started to get out of his chair. And I said that we'd still sue him for the five thousand, because nothing was said about getting it back in as-new condition and we'd all swear that it had already been bent when you recovered it.'

She kissed me on the bald spot and departed. Reverently, I watched her backside sway out through the doorway. Were I a more gifted writer, I could still never do full justice to those exquisite curves. I had always known that Alice's behind was one of the great beauties of nature. A thousand sonnets had been written, praising lesser charms. But I had never before realised just how valuable a weapon she could make of it.

Hammond
  Stray shot.

0 0 6 0 4 7 3 5 2 C.2